God's
Gift

Also by Dee Henderson
in Large Print:

Danger in the Shadows
The Negotiator (Also published in Spanish
    as el Negociador)
The Guardian
The Truth Seeker
The Protector
True Devotion
True Valor
True Honor
True Courage

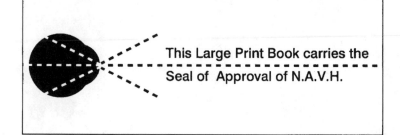

This Large Print Book carries the
Seal of Approval of N.A.V.H.

God's Gift

Dee Henderson

Walker Large Print • Waterville, Maine

Copyright © 1998 by Dee Henderson

Published in 2005 by arrangement with Harlequin Books S.A.

The text of this Large Print edition is unabridged.
Other aspects of the book may vary from the original edition.

Set in 16 pt. Plantin by Al Chase.

Printed in the United States on permanent paper.

The Library of Congress has cataloged the Thorndike Press® edition as follows:

Henderson, Dee.
    God's gift / by Dee Henderson.
      p. cm.
    ISBN 0-7862-7637-1 (lg. print : hc : alk. paper)
    ISBN 1-59415-086-9 (lg. print : sc : alk. paper)
    1. Missionaries — Fiction.   2. Chicago (Ill.) — Fiction.
  3. Wounds and injuries — Patients — Fiction.   4. Large type books. I. Title.
PS3558.E4829G63 2005
    813'.54—dc22   2005006675

Take delight in the Lord,
And He will give you
the desires of your heart.
Commit your way to the Lord;
Trust in Him, and He will act.
— Psalms 37:4–5

As the Founder/CEO of NAVH, the only national health agency solely devoted to those who, although not totally blind, have an eye disease which could lead to serious visual impairment, I am pleased to recognize Thorndike Press★ as one of the leading publishers in the large print field.

Founded in 1954 in San Francisco to prepare large print textbooks for partially seeing children, NAVH became the pioneer and standard setting agency in the preparation of large type.

Today, those publishers who meet our standards carry the prestigious "Seal of Approval" indicating high quality large print. We are delighted that Thorndike Press is one of the publishers whose titles meet these standards. We are also pleased to recognize the significant contribution Thorndike Press is making in this important and growing field.

Lorraine H. Marchi, L.H.D.
Founder/CEO
NAVH

★ Thorndike Press encompasses the following imprints: Thorndike, Wheeler, Walker and Large Print Press.

Chapter One

"Go back to the States, rest, see the doctors, shake this bug and be back here at the end of August to take the Zaire project." His boss's words still rang in his ears. *Medical furlough.* The words dreaded by every missionary. Six years in the field in remote locations. He should feel lucky to have made it this long. He didn't.

James Graham moved down the aisle of the plane, following the other passengers, a heavy jacket bought in New York folded over one arm. It had been eighty-two degrees when he left the capital of Zaire yesterday afternoon. The pilot had announced Chicago was forty-five degrees and raining, a cold April evening.

The pain was bad tonight. It made his movements stiff and his face gaunt. He moved like an old man and he was only thirty-five. He wanted to be elated at being home, to have the chance to see his friends, his family. It had been six years since he had been back in the States. Pain was robbing him of the joy.

He would give a lot to know what bug had bit him and done all this damage. He would give a lot to have God answer his question, *Why?*

He stepped through the door to the airport terminal, not sure what to expect. His former business partner Kevin Bennett had his flight information. James had asked him to keep it quiet, hoping to give himself some time to recover from the flight before he saw his family. His mom did not need to see him at his worst. For fifteen years, since his dad died, he had been doing his best to not give her reason to worry about him.

James could still feel the grief from the day his mom had called him at college to gently let him know his father had died of a heart attack. He'd been ready to abandon college and move back home, step into the family business, but she had been adamant that he not. She had compromised and let him return for a semester to help, then told him to get on with his life. She had sold the family bakery and begun a profitable business breeding Samoyeds, a passion she had shared with his dad for years.

When he'd felt called six years ago to leave the construction business he and

Kevin had built, to use his skills on the mission field, his mom had been the first one to encourage him to go. She was a strong lady, a positive one, but she was going to take one look at him in pain and while she wouldn't say so, she was going to worry.

"James."

He turned at the sound of his name and felt a smile pierce his fatigue. Six years was a long time to miss seeing a best friend. "Kevin." He moved out of the stream of people toward the bay of windows that looked out over the runways.

They had been close friends for so long, the six years blinked away in a moment. His friend looked good. Relaxed. A little older. They had gone to high school together, played baseball as teammates, basketball as rivals, he on the blue squad, Kevin on the red. They had double-dated together and fought intensely over who would be number one and who would be number two in all the classes they shared in college.

"I won't ask how you're doing. You look like you did that time you fell off that roof we were replacing," Kevin remarked. "I'm glad you're back."

James smiled. "I had to come back just to meet your wife."

Kevin laughed. "I have no idea how I

ended up married before you did. You'll like Mandy."

"I'm sure I will. She got you to settle down before you were fifty."

"Without you around as my business partner, there was too much work to do without help. I hired Mandy's brother — he's good by the way — and before I knew it, I was thinking more about Mandy than I was about work. I know a good thing when I find it."

"I'm glad, Kevin."

"It's your turn now."

James smiled. "Later, Kevin. We need a few dozen more clinics built before I want to think about coming back to settle down." He had come to the conclusion early, having watched his parents and other close friends, that marriage took time, energy and focus if you wanted it to grow and survive, and unless you were ready to make that kind of investment, it was simply better to wait. He had at least fifty more clinics to build. On the days he wondered if he had made the right choice, he had only to flip open his wallet and look at the pictures of the children the clinics had saved to know that for now, he had made the right decision. He was a patient man who planned to live a long life. There would be time for a good marriage, someday, not now — not while there was work that needed his attention. "You were able to keep my arrival quiet?"

"They think you were delayed by visa problems in Zaire. They aren't expecting you until late tomorrow."

"Thanks." James rolled his shoulders, hating the pain that coursed through his body and up his spine, making every bone ache. "An hour ride should give me time to let another round of painkillers take effect."

"Do the doctors know what made you ill?"

"No. It was probably an insect bite. They don't know what it is, but they're of the opinion that it will eventually run its course. I think Bob kicked me back to the States just to get me out of his office. He knows I hate a desk job."

He had told Bob to replace him. In the remote areas where the crews worked, it was critical that every man be able to pull his own weight — lives depended on it. They couldn't have a man who winced every time he swung a hammer managing a crew, no matter how intensely he wanted to keep the job.

James could tell that Kevin understood how deeply he had felt the loss; it was there in his eyes. He was grateful it wasn't pity.

"Fifteen weeks of your mom's good cooking, a baseball game or two and you will be back in Africa swinging a hammer, pouring cement, and wondering why you were crazy enough to go back."

The house had been painted, the color of the shutters changed from dark green to dark blue, the flower beds extended along the length of the house as his mom had planned. He had grown up in this house, built in a subdivision of similar homes, the asphalt driveway going back to the garage the place of many impromptu basketball games. His dad had liked to play and James had liked the chance to razz him about getting old. James felt a deep sense of peace settle inside. He had really missed this place.

Kevin pulled into the drive behind a blue Lexus. James glanced at the car, impressed. His transportation for the last six years had been four-wheel drive trucks. He had always appreciated a nice car.

"I'll bring in the bags," Kevin offered.

"Thanks," James replied absently, stepping out of the car and looking closer at the house. In the evening twilight he could see the porch still needed the third step fixed; it slanted slightly downward on the left end, and it looked as if the gutters were reaching the age when they should be replaced. He made a mental note to look at the window casings and check the roof, see what kind of age the shingles were showing. The grass was going to need to be mowed in another few weeks; he would have to make sure the mower blade was sharpened. The thought of being useful again felt good.

"Looks like your sister is here, that's her van."

"The Lexus?"

Kevin shook his head. "Don't recognize it. You were the one who remembers cars."

James led the way up the walk. "Do you still have my old Ford?"

"Runs like a dream. You would never know it's got a hundred eighty thousand miles on it. It's yours if you want it for the summer."

"Thanks, I might take you up on that. You must have found a good mechanic."

Kevin laughed. "With you gone, I had to."

James quietly opened the front door.

His mom had redone the entryway with new wallpaper, a modern design with primary colors and bold stripes. The hardwood floors were slightly more aged but polished until they gleamed. The living room to the right had white plush carpet and new furniture, a gorgeous couch and wing-back chairs. The place was filled with light even though it was now dark outside, the room warmed by a crackling fire in the fireplace. A CD was playing country music.

The house smelled of fresh-baked bread.

There were puppies sleeping in front of the fire on a colorful braided rug. Two of them, white fluffy bears that were maybe three months old. They reminded James of the little polar bears he had seen in the Coca-Cola commercial on the flight home.

"James!"

His sister Patricia was coming down the stairs, had reached the landing when she saw him.

He met her at the base of the stairs with a wide smile, a motion to lower her voice, a deep, long hug. His ribs ached where she hugged him back, but he ignored the pain as best he could. He had missed her, his companion in mischief. "You've gotten even more beautiful," he said, holding her at arm's length to look at her. Her hair was longer and her face serene for being the mother of two children. Paul must be fulfilling his promise to keep her happy.

She laughed, her eyes wet. "What are you doing here today? We weren't expecting you

14

till tomorrow."

"I like surprises," he replied, grinning. "Where's Mom?"

His sister returned the grin. "In the kitchen. She's been so excited at the idea of seeing you."

"James, I'll leave you to the family. Call me tomorrow?" Kevin asked, touching his arm.

James smiled and reached out a hand. "I will. Thanks, Kevin." He meant it more than he knew how to put into words.

James caught his sister's hand and pulled her with him down the hall to the kitchen at the back of the house. He had snuck down these halls as a kid to raid the refrigerator during the night, and had spent a good portion of his teenage years sitting at the kitchen table dunking cookies in his coffee, telling Mom about the day's events. Unlike most of his friends, he had loved to bring girlfriends home to meet his mom.

He leaned against the doorpost and watched his mom as she cleaned carrots at the chopping board. He felt tears sting his eyes. "Is there enough for one more?"

Mary spun around in surprise at his words and he saw the joy he felt mirrored in her face. The knife clattered down on the cutting board.

He steadied them both as her hug threatened to overbalance them, then leaned back to get a good look at her. "Hi, Mom."

"You rat. You should have told me your flight was today."

She had aged gracefully. He grinned. "And ruin the surprise?"

He stepped farther into the kitchen, his arm around her shoulders. "What's for dinner?"

"Vegetable soup, beef Wellington, fresh asparagus."

"And maybe apple pie," added a voice touched with soft laughter from his left.

James turned. The lady was sitting on the far side of the kitchen table, a bag of apples beside her. She was wearing jeans and a Northwestern sweatshirt, her hair pulled back by a gold clasp, her smile filled with humor. The black Labrador he had entrusted to his mom when he moved to the mission field was sitting beside her.

The lady was gorgeous. She gestured with her knife toward the peels she had been trying to take from the apples as an unbroken strand. "Your mom swears this is possible, but you're not supposed to arrive till tomorrow, so I have time to find out."

James grinned at the gentle rebuke. "It's all in the wrist," he remarked as he moved toward her.

"Rachel Ashcroft. Most people call me Rae. Your mom is giving me a baking lesson," she said lightly, holding out her hand.

James took her hand and returned her smile with one of his own. Rachel the Angel. His building crew had named her better than they knew. "Mom's a good teacher."

"And I'm a challenging student," she replied with a grin. "It's nice to finally meet you, James."

He liked the sound of her voice, the fact his mother liked her. Baking lessons were more than an act of kindness, they were a hallmark back to the days of the bakery and James knew his mom didn't just offer lessons to anyone.

He tugged a chair out at the table and turned it so he could stretch his legs out and greet his dog. The Labrador was straining to push his way into his lap, his tail beating against the table leg. "Easy, Jed, yes, it's me," James told the animal, stroking his gleaming coat, glad to see at fifteen years that Jedikiah appeared to still be in good health.

Rae leaned over to look past him. "Patricia, he's not nearly as tall as you claimed," she said in a mock whisper.

Patricia laughed as she pulled out the

chair between them. "Now that he's here, he's not nearly as perfect as we remember."

"Rae, I think the problem is he's been gone long enough I've forgotten all the mischief he use to get into," his mom said with a twinkle in her eye as she brought over a glass of iced tea for him. She lightly squeezed his shoulder. "It's good to have you home, James."

"It's mutual, Mom," he said softly, smiling at her, relaxing back in the chair. His journey was over for now.

It felt good to be home.

"Rae, you mean to tell me you actually volunteered for the junior high lock-in?" James teased.

They were stretched out in the living room enjoying the fire and relaxing after a wonderful dinner. His mom was beside him on the couch and his sister was sitting in the wing-back chair to his left. His dog was curled up at his feet. Rae was wrestling with the two puppies over ownership of a stretched-out sock.

"Staying up all night was no big deal. Patricia just forgot to tell me I would also be fixing breakfast for twenty junior high kids. Your niece, Emily, saved me. She's great at making pancakes."

"Let me guess . . . you taught her, Mom?"

"She's a natural," his mom replied, smiling.

A pager going off broke into the conversation. Rae glanced at the device clipped on her jeans. "Excuse me." She reached across the puppies to retrieve her purse and a cellular phone.

"Hi, Scott."

She listened for a few moments, the animation in her face changing to a more distant, focused expression. "How many Yen? Okay. Yeah, I'm on my way in. See you in about twenty minutes."

She closed the phone, got to her feet. "Sorry, I've got to go. Thanks for the baking lesson and dinner, Mary."

"Any time Rae. I enjoyed having you here."

"Call me about this weekend, Rae, maybe we can do lunch after church," Patricia asked.

Rae nodded. "Let me see what is on my schedule."

James saw the uncertainty in her eyes as she pulled on her jacket, glanced at him. "I'm sure we'll be seeing each other again," he commented with a smile. If he had anything to say about it, they would be. . . .

19

She gave a slight smile. "Probably. Good night, James."

"Good night, Rachel."

The drizzling rain made the road black and the streetlights shimmer as she drove to the office. Rae's hands were tense around the wheel, for the night reminded her too much of the one on which her partner Leo had died.

She had been in New York when their mutual friend Dave called, pulled her out of a pleasant dream and abruptly flung her into the harsh reality of Leo's death. Dave had chartered a plane to get her back without delay, and her girlfriend Lace had been waiting at O'Hare to meet her.

There hadn't even been time to grieve during the following ten days. Days after Leo's death, the markets began a ten percent fall. Rae, trying to learn to trade with Leo's skills overnight, felt crushed under the stress. Yet, it had been good, that crushing weight of work; it had insured she had a reason to get up each morning, a reason to block out the pain and focus on something else.

Her friends were good and loyal and there for her. She had survived. Part of her anyway. Part of her had died along with Leo that cold, wet, October night.

The mourning had started a few weeks later, the blackness blinking out her laughter for over a year.

She had promised Dave and Lace she would start getting out more. She knew they were worried about her; it had been eighteen months since Leo's death, but it still felt like yesterday. She wondered at times if the pain was ever going to leave.

In some respects, she knew the pain was a blessing. She had been to the bottom, the pain could not get worse. No matter what the future held for her, there was a certain comfort in knowing she had touched the bottom and she had survived. Life could offer her nothing worse than what she had already tasted.

She was picking up her life again, resuming activities she had enjoyed before Leo's death. She had begun to bowl on a league again, was back as a sponsor with the youth programs at her church, had decided to try once again to learn how to cook. She pursued the activities though the enjoyment was still hollow.

Tonight had been nice, relaxing, if a little intimidating to meet the man everyone spoke of so highly.

James Graham had been in pain tonight.

He had downplayed his answers to his mother's questions, but Rae had observed and drawn her own conclusions. He had moved with caution, as if expecting the pain.

She had seen Leo through too many broken bones and pulled muscles; she knew how unconscious movement was, how easily you moved first without thinking and then were caught by surprise. James had been living with pain so long, he had re-learned how to move.

He was worried. She had seen it in his face when he thought no one was watching. It had made her wish she could do something, anything to help. She hated to see someone suffer.

He had the guest room on the east side of the house. The shadows of the oak tree outside his window danced across the ceiling as cars passed by on the street below. The bed was comfortable, more comfortable than any he had slept in for the past six years.

He couldn't sleep.

His body was too exhausted, his muscles too sore.

James watched the play of shadows across the ceiling, absently flexing his right wrist where the pain was unusually intense. He had learned many weeks ago that it did no good to try to fight the fatigue. Eventually, sleep would come. Still, he knew he would feel exhausted when he woke, no matter how many hours his body slept.

It had been a good evening. He couldn't remember when he had enjoyed an evening or someone's company more.

Rachel the Angel. His crew in Africa had given her the name because of the packages she sent twice a month via Patricia. It had taken James almost four months to get an answer from Patricia on who was taping the Chicago Bulls basketball games for them. They had rigged up a battery powered TV/VCR to travel with them so they could enjoy the games.

Those tapes had been like water to his thirsty men. His crew had been mostly short-term help — college graduates and missionary interns there only for a specific building project. They had all been home-sick for something familiar. Rachel had no idea how important those gifts had been to him and his men.

He owed her a sincere thank-you.

He had watched her over dinner and as she had played with the puppies later. He had watched her when her face was relaxed and when she smiled.

She wasn't all she appeared to be on the surface.

Rae had been friendly, polite, and slightly flustered at the idea of interrupting a family reunion by staying for dinner. But the lightness and the laughter and the smile she had shown this evening had seemed forced. When she laughed, it didn't reach her eyes.

James had seen grief tempered by time before. He knew he was seeing it again.

The picture on the nightstand was the last thing Rae saw before she turned off the bedside light. Leo, his arm thrown around her, grinning. They had just won the skiing competition at Indian Hills. Their combined times for the run had put them in first place. Rae had to smile at the memory. He had forgotten to tell her how to slow down.

Hanging by a slender ribbon looped over the corner of the frame was the engagement ring Leo had bought her.

It was after 2:00 a.m. The Japanese stock market had gone into a decline and the rest of the overseas markets had followed it down. She had spent hours at her office deciding strategy for the opening of the New York markets. She could feel the tension and the stress through her body as she tried to cope with what she knew the coming day was going to be like.

She had never missed Leo more.

Leo had loved the trading, thrived on it; she just felt the fear. There was an overwhelming number of decisions to make rapidly, simultaneously, and it wasn't a game you could prepare for ahead of time, you just had to react to the markets and sense when to move in and out and when to hold and sweat it out. She would be back at her desk in three hours; she already wanted to throw up. She had never felt so angry at someone for dying as she did at Leo now.

Rae blinked back the tears and rolled onto her side to look at the moon visible over the trees.

God, why did Leo have to die? Why did he have to be driving too fast? If he hadn't chosen that road, at that time, he would be here tonight, as my husband, sound asleep beside me. He would be looking forward to facing the markets tomorrow, instead of dreading it.

God, I miss him so much. Is this ever going to end?

Please, I can't afford to play "I wish" tonight. I need some sleep. I need the ability to act decisively and with speed tomorrow. There are thirty clients depending on my actions, and six employees who are going to be taking their cues from me. I'm going to need Your help to-

morrow. Remember me, Lord. I'm depending on You.

Chapter Two

✝

"Lace, I've got too much work to do. I can't afford the time to go with you guys on vacation."

It was Saturday and Lace had come over early to drag Rae out of the house for a walk down to the park and back. Rae had groused about being woken up on the one morning she could sleep in, but now followed Lace down the path with the loyalty of a friend reluctantly conceding defeat. By the time she had convinced Lace she really should be allowed to sleep in, she had already been fully awake.

As she brushed her hair before the mirror, pulling it back into a ponytail, she noticed dark circles under her eyes. She heard Lace in the kitchen.

Rae didn't know what Lace had hoped to find. There was nothing left in the house. She had taken the last of the saltines to work with her to try to settle her stomach, ordered in food there when she got hungry. It had been an eighty-hour work week and it was only Saturday. She needed sleep, not exercise.

She had survived. It was the only good thing she could say about the week. The managed funds had crept up 1.24 percent against an index that had dropped two percent. She had traded her way out of the correction quite admirably.

Lace had insisted they stop for breakfast before they walked to the park. She had also frowned at the sweats Rae wore, but hadn't pushed it. Lace was saving her energy for another round of negotiations about their vacation.

They had been going on vacation together ever since their college days — Leo, Rae, Lace and Dave, plus whoever else they could tempt to come along. Rae loved the week in the country, fishing, hiking, relaxing. She just didn't see how it was possible to go this year; it had not been possible last year, and fundamentally, nothing had changed.

"Jack wouldn't mind coming out of retirement for a week to keep tabs on the accounts."

"Lace, it's not that simple."

The path widened and Lace dropped back beside her.

"Make it that simple. Rae, if you don't slow down, you're going to burn out. Do you honestly think Leo would have wanted this?"

Rae stopped walking, blinking away the unexpected tears.

"I'm sorry. I didn't mean to touch a raw memory," Lace said, her arm slipping around Rae's shoulders.

Rae nodded, knowing it was true. There was deep sympathy in her friend's eyes; Lace would hand over part of her own heart if she thought it would cure the pain. "I'm doing exactly what I have to, Lace. Keeping the business together while I look for a new partner to replace him. And you are right. Leo thrived on the day-to-day trading. For me, it's nerve racking. But I'm not working any harder than he did."

"He took breaks, Rae. You don't. If you don't stop soon, you're going to crash. Please, you need to come with us on vacation this year."

"The bridge games are just not the same without you," Lace added when Rae hesitated, dragging a smile from her. "Tell me you will at least think about it?"

Rae hugged her friend back and started walking down the trail again. "If I say no, is Dave going to be showing up at my door?"

"Now, would I do that?"

They had been best friends since Rae was nine years old, the year Rae's parents had died and she had come to live with her grandmother. Lace had lived down the street. They had a lot of history between them. Rae didn't buy the look of innocence. "Yes, you would."

They walked together down to the park benches where mothers could watch their children play on the swings and slides and rocking horses. Rae sat down, annoyed to admit to herself she was tired; Lace joined her on the bench. Her friend was fit and active and had the stamina to go for hours. Rae just felt old. She kicked a bottle cap on the rocks in front of the bench and watched it flip over, tilting her head to read the words inside.

"Dave says he's going to make senior partner next month."

Rae looked up in surprise. "How? The senior ranks are age sixty plus, he's thirty-six."

"He snagged some major client, and the firm is worried about the message it conveys to have a simple 'partner' working such a major account."

Rae laughed and the sound was rusty but felt good. "He got the Hamilton estate."

"Hamilton Electronics?"

"That's the one."

Even Lace looked impressed, and she didn't impress easily.

"When is he getting back from Dallas?" Rae asked.

"Tonight. I told him I would meet his flight."

Dave McAllister stepped off the plane from Dallas, and with a thank-you and generous tip accepted the sheaf of faxes and the ticket a courier was waiting to hand him. Then turned his wrist to glance at his watch. He had thirty-eight minutes before his flight to Los Angeles, barely time to find his luggage, get it on the right plane and check his messages, certainly not time for dinner.

There were days he hated being this good a lawyer.

"You eat, I'll read."

"Lace." He felt the relief at seeing a friend's face. She fell in step beside him, took the briefcase and papers, and handed him a chili dog. He didn't even protest the onions and eating a chili dog in a suit. She was a lifesaver. You didn't protest a lifesaver. Not at ten o'clock on a Saturday night.

"Jan told me about your abrupt arrive

and depart schedule."

There was amusement in her voice. Any time now she would be telling him to get a real life. He liked her too much to care. It was business. Sometimes it demanded a little sacrifice.

"Read me the important stuff," he asked her, finishing the chili dog and wishing she had bought him two.

She was flipping pages as they walked. "Oh, here's a good one." She skimmed the legal document with the ease of someone who wrote a lot of them. "Your client Mr. York is going to lose his shirt." She summarized the brief for him as they took the tunnel from terminal C to baggage claim.

"It's smoke. They are going to ask to settle out of court."

Lace grinned. "No, they won't."

"If they do settle, you owe me for that parking ticket you managed to pick up on my car."

He found his luggage and wished he had thought to pack for a longer trip. He hadn't been planning this trip to Los Angeles.

"Is Rae going to come?" It was the reason Lace had met him, the reason they had been playing phone tag across the country for the last several weeks.

"I got nowhere. You would think after

twenty years, I would know how to convince her to budge, but the only thing I managed to do was make her cry."

Dave frowned. "Lace, you were suppose to be helping, not making matters worse." He saw the look on Lace's face and lightened up, fast. He was going to have Lace crying, and one lady in his life in tears was enough. "She's having a down week, Lace, the markets turned, I bet it was nothing you said. She cried on me one time because I wore a tie like the one she had given Leo."

Lace blinked and put her lawyer face back on. "Good save, not great, but good. You're her silent partner, you've got to do something."

"Give me a clue what to do, and I'll do it. Anything," Dave replied, frustrated at the situation, frustrated at not being able to help one of the two most important friends he had left. "But I'm just as much at a loss as you are."

Lace nodded. "She's got to come on this vacation. That I do know."

Dave sighed. "Okay, I'll see what I can do when I get back to town Tuesday." He checked the monitors to find the gate for his next flight. "What are your plans for the rest of the week?"

"Sports stadium zoning and salary cap

contract language."

"Sounds like a whale of a good time."

She elbowed him in the ribs. "Beats playing divorce attorney. I thought you were going to get on the happy side of marriage for a change."

"I'm working on it, Lace," Dave replied, tweaking a lock of her hair. "Want to have dinner Thursday before Rae's game?" They were Rae's acting cheerleader section on nights she bowled with the league. It gave them an excuse to try to make her laugh again.

"Not Thai again, or Indian. I don't mind spicy, but I draw the line at curry."

"Need some help?"

The church nursery was busy with activity as one service finished and another prepared to begin. There were name tags to match with diaper bags and parents for children being picked up; new infants and diaper bags and instructions to write down for children being dropped off. Short-handed because two of the helpers were out with the flu, Rae was finally sitting down again. She looked up at the question and smiled.

James.

He looked good.

The unexpected thought made her blush, which really confused her and changed her smile to a momentary frown.

She looked down at the active infants she held. She had to grin. They were twins and she had her hands full. "Which one do you want?"

She watched him step into the nursery, careful to avoid letting any of the toddlers get past him and out the door. His movements were stiff and she wished their prayers on his behalf would be answered. She hated to see someone in pain. His week back in the States had faded his tan slightly. He sat down in the rocker beside her. "Give me —" he paused to read the name tags on their sleepers "— Kyle."

Rae carefully handed him the infant, watched him accept the six-month-old with the ease of someone comfortable around kids. The infant was fascinated with a man to look at.

"Patricia said I would find you here."

"I hide out here most Sundays," Rae replied, tempting Kyle's sister Kim with a set of infant car keys. She had been keeping up with infants and toddlers for the last hour and a half with her teenage helpers. She couldn't believe he'd shown up here of all places. She pushed her hair back as Kim reached for it again.

"Like kids?"

"Babies," Rae replied matter-of-factly.

"They grow up fast. Emily was barely walking when I saw her last. Now she's reading," James commented.

"Six years is a long time."

Rae snagged an infant who was in danger of falling backward and scooted him over to lean against her knee. James nudged a ball over to him with his foot.

"Thanks."

"It is always this lively?"

Rae smiled. "No one is crying so this is calm. But I normally do have two more adults to help keep order. They're both out with the flu. Thanks for the offer to help."

"My pleasure. I wanted to thank you for the Chicago Bulls tapes."

She was surprised and pleased that he had sought her out for something so simple. "Kevin said you were a fan."

"Your packages would make my week and that of my entire crew."

She looked down at the infant she held, embarrassed. "I'm glad you liked them."

"I'm afraid I've been thinking about you for two years by your nickname," James added.

His remark made her look up. "Really?"

He smiled. "We named you Rachel the Angel."

Now she really blushed. "They were just game tapes."

"They meant a lot to us. I promised the guys I would convey their thanks." James set the rocker in motion.

Rae had no idea what to say. "Should I apologize for not liking hockey?"

Her question brought a burst of laughter.

Rae left work Monday night after nine, stopped at the grocery store for a deli pizza and a six-pack of soda, and on impulse picked up a carrot cake. She needed to grocery shop to actually stock her cabinets but didn't have the energy.

She had decided she really, desperately, wanted a break. She was going to read a good book tonight, set her alarm to let her sleep an extra half hour and try to rebuild her energy. It was bad when she started the week exhausted.

She put the pizza in the oven, forgot and then came back to set the timer, walked down to the den as she poured the soda over ice. She wrinkled her nose and chuckled softly as she tried to drink around the fizz. She was parched.

Work would not be so bad if it were

simply not so long. She had given up trying to record her hours in February; tracking her time had been one of her New Year's resolutions. Knowing she was averaging 64.9 hours per week did not make coping with them any easier.

The library shelves were packed with books she considered worth keeping — thrillers and suspense and mysteries intermixed in the fiction, medical texts, financial texts and law references taking the rest of the space. She had a hard time choosing, there were so many books she would like to reread. She finally pulled down a hardcover by Mary Clark.

She settled into the recliner, kicking the footstand up. This was the way she liked to spend an evening.

She opened the book.

A small piece of red colored paper fluttered down between the arm and the cushion of the seat.

Rae shifted in the seat, balancing her drink and the book in one hand to reach the item.

A Valentine's Day card.

Leo's bold signature signed beneath his "I Love You."

The sob caught her off guard, emotion rushing to the surface before she could stop it.

No. No, she was done crying!

She wiped at the tears with the back of her sleeve, caught a couple deep breaths and forced them back. No. No more. She *was* done crying.

She got up.

It was hard, and her hand wavered, but she resolutely tucked the beautiful card in the box on the bookshelf where she kept the pictures she had yet to file in her scrapbook.

She wasn't going to let a card do this to her. It was beautiful, and there was no one to send her I Love You cards anymore, but she wasn't going to let the card affect her this way. No. She couldn't.

The desire to read was gone.

She left the book resting on the armrest of the recliner and returned to the kitchen. The pizza had barely begun to cook.

Was it possible to simply decide to stop grieving?

She leaned against the counter and watched the pizza cook.

Was it possible to simply decide not to grieve anymore?

Rae rubbed her burning eyes and reached to the medicine cabinet for the aspirin bottle. Her head hurt.

God, I've decided I'm not going to cry anymore. My head hurts, my eyes hurt, and crying over the fact I flipped open a book and had a Valentine's Day card he sent me fall out has got to stop. My life is full of reminders of him. He was in my life for ten years. He's there, in scrapbooks, in snapshots, in little knickknacks around the house. He fixed my car, and helped build my bookshelves, he even tried to teach me how to make pizza. Work is filled with reminders of him, he is there in every decision and in every stock position we hold. God, I'm not going to grieve anymore. You've got to take away the pain. But I'm through crying. He's gone.

She felt like she had been sideswiped by the same semi that had killed Leo.

When the pizza came out, she ate one piece and put the rest into the refrigerator, not hungry, not caring that she really needed to eat more than she had been in the last few months.

She took a hot shower and let the water fill the room with steam, cried her very last tears until she felt hollow inside, and quietly said goodbye.

She was going on with life. She only hoped it held something worth going on for.

"What do you think?" Kevin asked, leaning against the side of the construction trailer.

James looked out over the eighty acres of land Kevin was turning into a new subdivision of affordable homes and felt slightly stunned. "Kevin, you have done wonders with the business in six years."

His friend laughed. "Believe me, it has more to do with you than you realize. The early days of the business established such a high-quality standard that almost overnight the business opportunities began to come to us faster than we could meet them.

"It was that house we built for Ben Paulson that turned the corner. He considered the construction so top-notch, that when he began to put together this community, he approached us with the business."

"How's the business mix — new construction versus additions, reconstruction?"

"It's tipped sixty–forty toward new construction now. You want to take a look?" Kevin asked, motioning to the current homes being built.

"Please."

They walked across the site to one of the framed-in homes. "We have five basic models going up in this subdivision. Most are selling before we even pour the foundation. This is the most popular model. Three bedrooms, two baths, with an open great room."

"You've got a good architect."

Kevin stepped into the studded kitchen. "Not as good as you," he replied with a grin, "but Paul has an eye for both space and cost. He's been a good addition to the team."

Kevin stepped through what would someday be a patio door. "Of course partner, when you get tired of Africa, we've got a lot of work to do here."

James laughed. "I think you've got things well under control." He looked around the staked-out lots and thought about what this place would look like in five years, full of homes and families and kids, a place for dreams to be born. It felt good knowing the business here had thrived while the work in Africa had thrived as well. There were times when he could see God's hand at work and this was one of them. Instead of building only here, they were building both here and overseas.

The doorbell rang.

Rae was sprawled on the couch with the book that had come in the mail that day. It was Tuesday and it had been a long day. She had decided on the drive home that it was time to pick up the final part of life she had left idle since Leo's death, the book she had been working on. When she had found the package with the medical text waiting for her on her doorstep, it had solidified her decision.

She glanced at her watch. She wasn't expecting anyone.

With some reluctance, she put down the book and went to get the door.

"Dave." She was both surprised and pleased to see him.

"Dinner?" He was carrying a pizza box from the place down the street and his smile made her grin in reply.

"You angel. Sure. It's what? Only ten o'clock?" she teased.

"I just got off work, and it's time for congratulations."

"Oh? You won your case?"

He rolled his eyes. "You, my little friend. When were you going to call me?"

Her . . . oh, the stock that went public . . . Her smile widened. It had been such a long day she had actually forgotten. "It was only a little killing," she demurred.

"Sixty-four percent in one day. And you had an even hundred thousand on the line. I would have brought ice cream as well, but they were out of pralines and cream. You look good," he said, seriously.

She wasn't in the mood for serious tonight. "Thanks a lot, friend. Go get silver-ware, the game's on."

He moved around her town house with the ease of an old friend, finding plates and napkins, the pizza cutter he had put in her stocking last Christmas.

The living room coffee table had served as a table for many such late-night dinners. Dave discarded his suit jacket and tie, rolled up his sleeves, kicked off his shoes. He settled on the floor, using the couch as a backrest. "Who's winning?" The Chicago Bulls game was muted on the TV.

Rae handed him one of the sodas she had snagged from the bottom shelf of the refrigerator, helped herself to a slice of the thick-crust supreme pizza. "The Bulls are up by eight in the third quarter, the Sonics are having a bad night."

He nudged the book on the edge of the table around so he could see the title. "*Cell Microbiology*?"

"Research for my book," Rae commented easily, sinking back against the pillows she had pulled from off the couch. "This pizza is great. Thanks."

"No problem."

"What were you doing at the office till ten o'clock?"

"Some pro bono work. Yet another father

44

not fulfilling his child support obligations."

"Will he come through?"

Dave shrugged. "I can force it here as long as he doesn't go underground with a cash job or change states."

"You'll let me know what the family is short?"

Dave nodded. "The fund got enough cash?"

"Eight thousand. It will last about another ten weeks."

"Let me know when it runs dry. I'll match you again."

"Thanks."

Dave nodded.

Rae smiled quietly at her friend as he snagged the remote and turned the sound back on. They frequently supported families they knew were in financial need. He was as generous as she was, he just didn't like people to know it.

They watched the game and ate pizza, the silence between them that of old friends. "So, have you thought about coming with us?" Dave asked finally.

Rae laughed. "Lace sent you, didn't she?"

"Rae, you did not come last year. We understood. But you need a vacation. I'm not accepting any excuses this year. If I can get a week off, you can too."

"Dave, I've got new clients to deal with, a load of new stock issues to evaluate, and a market that's so high it makes me cringe. I can't afford to be gone a week."

"That is exactly why you have to come. There is never going to be a good time to take a break. When the markets are good, you're worried about them dropping, and when the markets correct, you're worried about losing other people's money. You're coming."

She tipped her soda can toward him. "When did you get so pushy?"

He chuckled. "Rae, I've always been pushy, you just like me too much to care."

Rae sighed. She had thought about the problem at length. She did want to go. . . . "I'll call Jack tomorrow and see if he's free." Jack had been Leo and her first backer in the business, and as an experienced stock-broker, she trusted him to keep the accounts stable while she was away from the office.

"He is. I already called him."

Rae chuckled. "I should have never given you that power of attorney." It had made sense at Leo's death to have another partner officially on the books in case something happened to her. Dave had been the natural choice.

"I'm your biggest backer, not to mention

one of your more wealthy clients. You have to listen to me," Dave replied with a grin.

She thumped him with a pillow. "I think it's time I get some new friends," she remarked and had to duck when a pillow came back at her.

"The doctor said fresh air and rest?"

"That's taking a little liberty with his prescription, but yes, that's essentially it. That, and some medication that is making the pharmacist rich." James was sitting at the dining room table at his sister's house, his chair turned and his legs stretched out before him, watching her finish clipping pictures for the Sunday school class she taught. He had managed to sleep until ten and for once had awoke with some energy and only moderate pain. Either the medicine or the downtime were helping. He had eaten lunch with Mom then come over to see Patricia and the kids.

"Then camping fits the bill. Come with us."

"Patricia, it hardly seems right to invite myself along on your vacation."

"Nonsense. The cabin can easily sleep ten, and we had planned the food assuming Paul was going to be able to come. Since he can't, you might as well take his place." His sister nodded toward the window. "The kids would relish having you around for an entire week."

James motioned his coffee cup toward the kids. "Last night you were worried about them wearing me out," he replied with a twinkle in his eyes.

Patricia grinned. "That was before I knew Paul was flying to Dallas. You're new, male and a relative. They will listen to you. I'm just Mom."

He laughed. "Ahh. Kid patrol. I get it."

"Seriously, you wouldn't have to do anything but sleep in, eat wonderful food and watch a bobber. It would do you good."

"What are the odds there are bugs that bite?" he asked, smiling. He had already made the decision to go, he just liked making his sister work for it.

"I will personally tell even the mosquitoes to leave you alone," she promised.

He set down his coffee cup and absently rubbed his aching wrist. "What do I need to pack?"

"Yes!" Her eyes danced with delight and he laughed.

"The days are comfortable but the nights can be a little chilly since we are beside the lake. I would bring whatever you want to read, the selection there is eclectic and quite old."

Now he had reason to laugh. "You just described a weekend on a building site, Patricia."

His sister grinned. "Then it will feel like home."

Chapter Three

✞

"I can't believe you talked me into this."

Dave tossed her suitcase in the trunk.

"A vacation will do you good," he replied, reaching over to drop a college cap he had snagged from his bag onto her head. "Lighten up. You're officially on seven days of R and R. Besides, it's Memorial Day Weekend."

She wrinkled her nose at him and adjusted the cap. "Dave, my idea of a camping trip is slightly different than yours. I suppose you brought that jazz CD for the trip again, didn't you?"

"It's tradition."

"You don't like jazz. You just don't have the heart to tell Lace that."

He blushed slightly. "It was a birthday gift. One that I appreciate," he stressed.

Rae grinned. "Why don't you just ask her out and end her misery?"

"And ruin a great friendship?" He rolled his eyes. "Please, you've got to be kidding."

She pushed him aside to rearrange the bags he had crammed in the trunk. "You're just gun-shy about making a commitment. It's past time you got married, you know."

"Don't start acting like my mother, Rae. I've got a life I enjoy. The marriage bit can wait."

"You wait too much longer friend, and she's going to find someone else," Rae replied. She gestured to the walk. "Bring me that black bag next."

He picked it up and the smaller one beside it, giving her a dirty look. "A few books you said? You're taking your entire library."

"I told you my idea of a vacation was different than yours. I plan to sleep, read and do some writing."

"No fishing?"

She took the smaller bag from him. "I might drown a worm if you promise nothing will bite it."

She reached for the other bag, but he held it back.

"This feels like a computer. . . ."

She put her hands on her hips and grinned at him. "Don't push it, David, you'll lose the argument."

He handed it over. "Am I going to get nagged into finding you a copy of the *Wall*

Street Journal every morning?"

"I'll read it on-line," she replied, slipping the laptop into a cushioned spot between her jacket and his. "Okay, let's pick up Lace."

"Mind if I relegate you to the back seat for the trip?"

Rae grinned. "I thought you said you weren't interested?"

"You're just going to stick your nose into a book. Lace likes my jokes."

Rae laughed. "There are some she likes just about as much as you like jazz."

"She laughs."

"She's got a sweet heart. And if you break it, I'm going to make your life miserable," Rae replied.

"Rae?"

The question nudged her away from her research. "Hmm?"

"We're going to stop at the welcome station and get new state maps. You want us to bring you a box of their free popcorn?"

Rae shifted the pen she had clutched between her teeth. "Sure. While you're there, check and see if they have new maps of the lake. They were planning to update them to show the new trails."

"Okay."

It was almost four in the afternoon. Lace and Dave had been chatting for most of the drive. Rae had lost track of the conversation a couple of hours ago.

She stretched her back and considered putting her research notes and books back in order. The cabin was about thirty minutes away now. A glance at the spine of the book showed she had more than a hundred pages still to read in this latest medical textbook.

She should have become a doctor.

Yawning, she slipped her page marker into the book and closed it, reached over and slipped it back into her briefcase.

The actual manuscript she was working on was in her suitcase, the three hundred pages too hefty for her briefcase. Writing was her one persistent hobby. Crafts, sewing, watercolors had come and gone over the years; she always came back to her writing. She was getting better. Lace and Dave both liked this story. Leo had liked it so much he'd tried to convince her to cut back her hours at the office so she could finish it.

She wanted to finish the novel and write a dedication page to Leo. She thought it might be a way to help her say goodbye.

She smiled. She wouldn't mind seeing her

name on the spine of a published book, either. For all this effort, there should be some payback.

She felt lighter in spirit than she had in the last year. They were right. The vacation was going to do her some good. She was looking forward to days not driven by the markets, a chance to read for pleasure, the freedom to sleep in, the right to be lazy.

The edge to the grief was beginning to temper. The sadness was still there, heavy, and so large it threatened to swamp her, but the pain was less. She had prepared for the vacation. She knew it was going to be hard, not having Leo with them, not having him there for the game, or messing up the kitchen with his creations, or dragging her hiking.

It was going to be okay.

She should have picked up working on the book months ago. It was good, and when she worked on it, she felt better than she had in a long time.

She was determined to smile, laugh, and do her best to have a good time.

"Emily is asleep."

James glanced in the rearview mirror to see his niece collapsed against the bright yellow Big Bird pillow she had brought with her. He smiled at his nephew Tom, sitting in the front passenger seat. "It was only a matter of time. Your mom was asleep hours ago."

"She was up late with Dad," Tom replied. "They've been talking about having another baby."

James choked. "Do you want a brother or sister?" he asked, trying to keep his voice neutral.

"Sister. That way Emily will stay out of my stuff and have another girl to play with."

It was a big deal when you were nine.

"I hear your dad has been coaching you for the football team."

"He's trying. I still can't throw a spiral. Jason can, and he makes a big deal out of it."

"You'll get it with more practice."

"Want to play catch with me?"

James flexed his aching ankle and was grateful the van had cruise control. "I'd be glad to, Tom."

"Thanks. Mom doesn't catch very well."

James grinned. "She never could. I spent years trying to teach her how to catch a baseball."

"She says she was pretty good."

"It's relative, Tom. She was pretty good

for a girl who shut her eyes when the ball got close."

Tom grinned. "She does that with a football, too." He grimaced. "I hit her in the face one time by accident. She wasn't very happy."

James glanced back at Patricia, curled up awkwardly in the back seat with her head tucked against her jacket and a pillow. "She's your mom. I bet she's forgotten all about it."

"I hope so. My birthday is next month."

James laughed.

"Check your mom's directions again, Tom. I see exit fifty-eight coming up."

Papers rustled as Tom found the map and the handwritten directions. "That's the one. Then take Bluff Road north for five miles. She'll have to direct from there. I know it's lots of trees and water."

"Got it."

Fifteen minutes later, the van pulled up in front of the vacation getaway.

It was a beautiful cabin, built at the top of a hill looking out over a calm lake that the map showed went for miles. They were half a mile from the nearest neighbor, and ten miles from town.

James stepped out of the van and stretched, fighting the pain in his spine that came from sitting too long, the muscles in his ribs aching with every breath he took. He smiled at the sound of birds. "Who did you say owned this place?" he asked Patricia.

"A friend of Dave's. There are a couple canoes and a fishing boat in the boathouse and a neighbor has horses he lets us ride."

Patricia pointed to the shoreline to the north. "Just around that bend is a large meadow and what is practically a sandy beach. It makes a great place to picnic. The fishing is good everywhere along this inlet. The kids were catching crappies off the end of the pier last year."

"It looks like we're the first to arrive. Do you have a key?"

"It's off the silver star on my key ring."

The porch was solid oak and extended around the cabin, the front door snug and smooth to open. James stepped inside and paused to enjoy the sight. The place had obviously been designed by an architect who knew his stuff. A large fireplace with open seating around it, a spacious kitchen, a large dining room, an encompassing view of the lake. The deck on the back of the house led down to a pavilion built beside the water.

He turned as Patricia came in with a bag of groceries. "This is going to be a good place to relax."

She smiled. "I'm glad you came."

She turned at the sound of another car. "That must be Dave and the others now."

"Lace, do you want the Wedding Ring quilt or the David's Star quilt?"

"The blue one," Lace replied from somewhere inside the massive walk-in closet.

Rae laughed. "They are both blue."

"Then you choose." Lace stepped back into the room, having hung up her clothes. "I do love the smell of cedar in a closet. You want me to unpack your suitcase?"

"Sure, though I doubt the jeans and T-shirts will care much where they are tossed."

"Didn't you bring anything nice?"

Rae grinned. "Why should I? I can borrow from you."

Lace groaned as she saw the contents of Rae's suitcase. "I'm going to get you fashion conscious if it takes my entire life to do it."

"Lace, face it. I've got a very limited sense of ascetics. If it's comfortable, I wear it." Rae pulled out the small bear Leo had given her and tossed it on her bed near her pillow. "You ready to eat? The guys are probably raiding the food even as we speak."

"Sure. We can walk it off tomorrow. Dave wants to try that trail that wanders up to the eagle viewing platform."

"A five-mile hike, mostly uphill, is not my idea of a good time," Rae replied.

She laughed at Lace's expression. Her friend had discovered the romance novel tucked in the side pocket of the suitcase.

"Want to borrow it after I'm done?"

Lace grinned and tossed it on the nightstand. "With two, good-looking, single guys on the premises? Why bother to read?"

Rae tugged Lace to the door. "Come on friend, there is mischief to make. I still owe Dave for that ice down my back two years ago."

Lace laughed. "The long arm of revenge is about to strike one unprepared man. What are you planning?"

"I have no idea. But that has never deterred me before."

James couldn't decide who he liked more, Lace or Rae. They were sprawled out on the floor battling it out over a checker board, both having soundly beat Dave an hour earlier.

Lace was the more outgoing of the two, Rae more contained and likely to be the one who smiled quietly. They were obviously old, lifelong friends.

No, it wasn't really a contest. Lace was nice, but Rae . . . Rae had him almost regretting he was going back to Africa in a couple months.

Dave dropped a new log on the fire and both ladies jumped. He ruffled Rae's hair. "Sorry. Want a toasted marshmallow if I get the stuff?"

"Sure."

Patricia came back and James slid over, gestured for her to put her feet up on the couch. She had finally convinced two worn-out kids that ten o'clock was late enough for bed. "Thanks, my feet are killing me."

"Maybe you should have passed on the game of tag."

She laughed. "And lose out on the opportunity to hug my son? It's worth a few aches."

James pushed off her tennis shoes and gently massaged her feet. Both her ankles were swollen. He smiled. He was almost positive she was pregnant.

He would be back in Africa when the child was born. His face tightened at the thought.

"Ribs still bothering you?" Patricia asked quietly.

"Not bad," James replied. The pain was tolerable. He'd live. "What's that you're eating?" he asked, noting the sandwich she had brought back with her.

She looked guilty. "Roast beef and hot mustard."

She was pregnant.

James grinned. "Next time you go scavenging for something to eat, I'll teach you how to make Manallies. You'll love them."

Lace won the checker game and Rae rolled over onto her back with a groan. "Lace, you are a devious, underhanded, world champion of world champions. What is that now, the last fifteen games we have played?"

"Leo could beat me," Lace replied, sliding the pieces back into the box.

"Leo could beat anyone at anything," Rae replied, pushing herself up and redoing the ponytail that was holding back her long hair.

Dave offered a golden toasted marshmallow. "Careful, it's hot."

Rae slipped it off the stick. "Thanks." She stood up. "Anyone need a drink? I'm going to go raid the ice chest."

"See if we've got another Sprite," Lace replied. Rae glanced at Dave who shook his head and at Patricia who indicated a soda at her feet, stopping at James with a raised eyebrow.

"Root beer."

She nodded. "Coming up."

She was gone a long time for someone simply getting sodas from the ice chest. She came back with three soda cans. She handed the Sprite to Lace. "Dave, you want to help me carry in more wood for the box? The radio said we might get some rain tonight."

"Sure. Be right there."

James caught a private byplay between Lace and Rae, saw a smile pass between them, and wondered if the guys should stick together. They *were* outnumbered two to one. Rae looked at him as she handed him the soda he had asked for; James decided Dave was on his own.

They disappeared out the front door and James saw Lace struggling to contain her laughter.

"Sorry, I've got to see this. It's two years overdue." Lace slipped over to the window to look out at the porch.

"What did he do?"

"Put ice down her back when she and Leo were dancing."

James glanced at his sister. "Who's Leo? He's been mentioned several times," he asked softly.

"Rae's business partner. He was killed in a car accident a year and a half ago," Patricia replied.

"They were close?"

"Yeah."

His heart tightened. No wonder he saw sadness behind Rae's smile.

There was a crash from the front of the house and the roar of a surprised man.

Lace was laughing. "Good job, Rae." She came back and dropped into one of the plush chairs. "We're going to need to get more ice," she remarked, reaching down to pick up her soda. "Dave is sitting in it."

Dave came in brushing water off the back of his jeans and shaking ice out of the back of his sweatshirt. "Rae, that was excessive," he mildly remarked, scowling at her as she slipped under his arm.

"That was two years of interest," she replied with a twinkle in her eyes. "You want a towel?"

He tweaked her ponytail. "Bring me two."

She came back with two bath towels, draped one around his shoulders. He took the other and rubbed under his sweatshirt.

"You know I owe you one now."

She laughed. "Got to catch me first."

She dropped into the chair opposite Lace. "Lace, he's got six days to retaliate. I think I should have waited a few days."

Dave came in carrying a soda and Rae

ducked when he stopped behind her chair, half-afraid she was going to get a bath with it.

James chuckled.

It was going to be quite a week around these three friends.

Chapter Four

✝

"Tranquil morning."

It was the crack of dawn. Rae, seated on the porch steps, turned, surprised. She knew neither Dave nor Lace were likely to be moving at this time of the morning.

James.

"Couldn't sleep?" she asked, concerned. He was in pain, she could see it in his movements and his face.

"Overdid it yesterday. I pay for mistakes like that," he replied, sinking down onto the porch steps beside her. "Thanks for making the coffee."

She smiled. "Not a problem. I don't wake up without it."

"These days, neither do I," he replied. "Why aren't you sleeping in?"

How was she suppose to answer that? The truth or something that made sense? Rae shrugged a shoulder, then changed her mind and decided to tell him the truth. "Ever have one of these experiences in life that just stops you in your tracks until you figure it out?"

She liked his smile and the frank way he turned and met her gaze. "Like God just grabbed your jacket collar, tugged, and said 'No, think about this'?" he asked softly.

Rae nodded. She drew her knees up and folded her arms around them. "I woke up about 2:00 a.m. with Psalm 37 running through my mind. I don't know why. Feels important."

He leaned back on his hands, his expression thoughtful. "It's an interesting Psalm. Trusting God with your dreams, the security He provides, the promise of refuge in times of trouble. What were you thinking about when you went to bed — if you don't mind me asking?"

Rae smiled at the room he was trying to give her. She didn't know if it was the conversation topic or the fact it was her that had him slightly uncomfortable. "Nothing earth-shattering. The book I've been writing."

He looked surprised. "I didn't know you were a writer."

"Have been for years. I'm not published, just enjoy doing it." She tipped her coffee cup to see if there was any left.

"Sounds like fun."

She smiled. "It's a different kind of work."

A blue jay dropped down past the porch steps to land on the flagstones and check out what looked like a dropped dime. He took back to flight with a raucous cry.

"Most of the time when a scripture comes to mind like you described, it's because it is an answer to a question you were asking."

The only thing I've been asking lately is where do I go now that Leo is dead. . . .

"Could be," she replied, knowing he was right. She nodded toward his coffee mug. "What some more? I need a refill." She didn't want to think about Leo and the past. Not on this vacation.

He knew. It was there in his eyes. He knew she was avoiding something God wanted her to deal with. He handed her the mug. "Sure," he said.

He'd probably never been afraid to face anything in his life. Rae wished she had that kind of courage. She didn't. Not when it came to saying goodbye to what she might have had. "Black?"

"Please."

When she came back out with the coffee, he had moved, stretched his legs out fully, was slowly working his right knee. He was doing his best not to grimace with the movement.

Rae felt an intense sense of empathy for him. He was like Kevin, a man accustomed to days of physical work. The pain had to be hard to cope with. She sat back down beside him, leaving a foot of space between them, turning slightly so she could lean against a porch post. "Patricia said the bug was damaging your joints," she remarked, handing him the refilled mug.

"It's doing damage like lupus, fibromyalgia, or the aggressive forms of arthritis. The joints lose the ability to move freely."

"Is it getting better?"

He grimaced. "At a snail's pace. They don't know what bug I picked up, and they don't know how long the symptoms are going to last."

"Is it the pain that messes up your sleep?" she asked, curious.

"Yes and no. The sleep study showed there is a lot of alpha wave activity during what should be delta sleep. My body isn't sleeping properly anymore. They don't know why."

"You weren't praying for patience by any chance, were you?"

He smiled. "I was praying for someone to

show up in Africa who knew how to train medical staff. We were building clinics faster than we could staff them."

"What's the problem with getting staff?"

"Money. Doctors who have been in practice for a few years have grown to like the income and don't want to go, doctors straight out of medical school are so deep in school debts, they can't afford to go."

"I don't know why that surprises me. We've got the same problem staffing the Crisis Centers here."

The door behind them opened. "Would you two like a hot or cold breakfast? We've got everything from fruit and cereal to bacon and eggs," Patricia asked.

"I want you to give me another pancake making lesson," Rae requested, scooping up her mug. "The squirrels can eat the ones I burn."

James laughed. "Rae, she's not the best at it either."

"She's better than I am. That's all I care about," Rae replied with a grin as they both went inside.

"Dave, Rae is *cooking*." It was a whispered warning overheard from the hall. James had to smile at Lace's reaction. No one could be that bad a cook.

He changed his mind thirty minutes later.

Rae had tried, but the pancakes were not like the ones his mom made.

Rae chuckled at the expressions on her friends' faces around the table, pulled back the plate of remaining pancakes she had set on the table and reappeared with a plate of pancakes Patricia had fixed. "I'm getting better, you didn't try to stifle a gag."

"Rae, why don't you just give up?" Dave asked. "It's not your fault your grandmother refused to cook. Cooking is something you either learn as a child or it's a lost art."

"Nope. I'm going to learn how if it kills me," she replied, helping herself to two of the pancakes Patricia had fixed.

"It might kill one of *us* one of these days," Dave replied, then yelped when someone kicked him under the table.

"David Hank McAllister, be nice."

"She knows I'm teasing, Lace."

"Hank?" Rae burst out laughing.

Dave turned to Lace. "Now see what you've done? You promised you wouldn't tell."

Rae's laughter intensified. "Hank. Oh this is rich."

"I'll give you rich, *Amy*."

Rae wrinkled her nose at him and did her best to stop her laughter. "I can't believe

I've known you ten years without knowing your middle name."

"What's so funny?" Emily had joined them, wiping sleep from her eyes. James lifted her up into his lap, his own laughter hard to contain. "Just adult stuff," he told her, smiling.

The threesome quieted down. "Sorry, Dave," Lace whispered, then giggled.

He snagged his coffee mug to get a refill, his head shaking as he walked to the kitchen. "Women."

Rae leaned across Dave's empty chair toward Lace, a smile dancing across her face. "I think I know what we should get him for his birthday."

Lace had to stifle her laughter at the whispered suggestion. "Think we could still find the CD?" Lace asked. "He hates country music almost as much as he does jazz. It's perfect."

"You knew?"

Lace grinned. "He hides a cringe every time I choose track four. He is so easy to get."

"Lace, you are good," Rae said, sitting back in her chair and looking at her friend with new respect.

Lace leaned back in her chair. "I'm better than good," she replied with a smile. "He's never going to know what hit him."

Laughter was good medicine, James thought. He hadn't felt this good in weeks. Watching Rae and Lace, he couldn't contain his smile.

Rae caught him watching her and grinned. "You'll get use to us, James."

"I'm enjoying it," he replied, watching her blush slightly.

Lace saw the blush and turned to look at him. He winked. James saw Lace hesitate a moment and glance back at Rae. Then a wide smile crossed her face. "Dave," Lace called, "we want to go canoeing this morning. But I'm riding with you. Rae sent me into the drink last time."

Dave appeared in the doorway, munching on a piece of bacon. "Only if I'm steering."

"You can steer," Lace agreed, getting up to clear her place.

"Lace, I wanted to lounge on the patio with a book," Rae remarked, stacking the plates.

"No, you don't. You want to go canoeing."

Rae looked at her friend, puzzled. "Okay." She glanced over at Patricia and James. "Either one of you want to go canoeing?"

"The kids and I have a date with a pair a

horses," Patricia replied, smiling.

"Can I steer?" James asked quietly.

Rae looked at him, finally caught the byplay between him and Lace, flushed, then laughed. "Sure." She snagged her friend's sweater. "Come on, Lace. You need to put those plates in the sink."

Lace let herself get tugged out of the room. "I need to put these plates in the sink," she agreed, winking back at James.

Dave watched them go with a rueful smile. He tugged out his chair with his foot. "It is going to be a *long* week."

James laughed. He had a feeling both he and Dave were going to enjoy it.

"Do you want to beach the canoe and rest your wrists for a while?"

James smiled. "Relax, Rae. I'm fine. That's the fourth time you've asked."

"You're here to recover, not make matters worse."

She rested her paddle across the bow and leaned over to watch a school of sunfish slide by near the surface.

She had a nice back. He'd been admiring the view for the last hour.

His wrists were sore, but not intolerable. His shirt was almost dry. There had been a laughter-filled water fight between the two canoes about forty minutes back. He hadn't felt this relaxed in months. Nothing to do but drift with the current and spend time with a beautiful lady.

The canoe way ahead of them rocked wildly and Rae ducked her head so as not to look. "Tell me she isn't trying to stand up."

James chuckled. "Okay, I won't."

Lace somehow managed to turn around without tipping the canoe over. "Want to catch up with them?" James asked.

Rae shook her head. "They are probably debating the ethics of civil litigation again. I'll pass."

"What does Lace do for a living, anyway?"

Rae resumed paddling, her movements sure and smooth. It added a slight sway to her back. "It's more a question of what she hasn't done. She's the daughter of a federal judge and a district attorney. She's got a law degree, but more because it's what the family does than anything else. She's forgotten more law than most lawyers ever learn. She doesn't like to settle down. She's worked in international banking, edited textbooks, worked for Senator White. She's currently doing some consulting work for a sports management firm downtown."

"Was that where you three met? College?"

"I've known Lace since I was nine. We met Dave and Leo at Northwestern. We made an awesome foursome. Dave the fighter for justice, Leo the energy, Lace the constant new interests, and me the practical planner."

James smiled. "You're also the hub they revolve around."

"That's because I'm always there doing the same thing," Rae replied with a smile. "I'm a creature of habit."

"You grew up with your grandmother?"

"My parents died in a car wreck when I was nine. We were living in Texas at the time. The next day this wonderful lady in her fifties appeared and said, 'Don't worry. You've still got me.' I had heard about her all my life, got Christmas presents and birthday gifts, but not seen her since I was about five. The day we arrived at her house in Chicago, five inches of snow fell. I thought I had moved to another planet."

James smiled. She had loved her grandmother a lot, he could hear it in her voice. He caught a glimpse of golden brown and dipped his paddle deep, turned the canoe twenty degrees to the left. "Look behind that fallen tree." A deer had come down to the water's edge to drink.

"She's beautiful," Rae whispered.

The animal raised its head, paused, then went back to drinking.

They watched for several minutes. The animal picked its way over driftwood, then slipped back into the woods.

"Want to try out those sandwiches Patricia sent?" There was a clearing up ahead of them.

Rae picked up her paddle. "Sure."

"So, did you have a good time?"

Rae rolled onto her side in the spacious bed, half smiled at the question from the other side of the dark room. "I can't believe you set me up."

"He's a nice guy."

Rae smiled in the darkness. "Yes, he is. He's also leaving the country in less than three months," she pointed out, being practical.

"That's tomorrow's problem," Lace replied. "It was good to see you enjoying yourself."

"Lace, I always enjoy a vacation."

"Not since Leo died."

Rae bit her bottom lip. "I really miss him, Lace."

"I know you do," came the soft reply. "You okay?"

It had been a nice day, but it had been

hard. The cabin was yet another place filled with memories of Leo. She had missed Leo's tap on the door, waking her up at 5:00 a.m. to go fishing, missed having him fix breakfast for them. She had enjoyed the afternoon with James. He didn't seem to mind the silence or the space she preferred. It was almost better, knowing he was going back to Africa — easier at least. The last thing she wanted to even consider was risking getting hurt again. "Yeah, I'm okay." She would be. When God helped her fix the hole in her heart. "Remember those canoe races Leo and Dave use to have?"

"Holding that rope across the water for a finish line was not one of our more well thought out actions," Lace replied.

Rae laughed softly. They had both been pulled into the water when the guys reached up and grabbed the rope. "They had to have been planning that one for weeks ahead of time."

"You got Dave good last night, by the way."

"Thanks. Watch my back for me, okay? I have no idea how he's going to retaliate."

"I'll do my best," Lace promised. " 'Night, Rae."

" 'Night, Lace."

Rae wished she had brought her jacket. It was late afternoon. The breeze coming up from the lake made it cool in the shade. She had hiked to the highest point near the cabin, a hill that let her look out over the water. They had been at the cabin for three days, and the slow, easy pace had taken away a sense of strain that she had not been aware she was carrying.

God, You know what Psalm 37 says. Take delight in the Lord, and He will give you the desires of your heart. I feel like that promise got broken.

The prayer was a soft one. Rae settled back against the trunk of a tree and watched the water.

. . . the desires of your heart . . . That's what she felt had been taken from her with Leo's death. She'd had a relationship with him, a deep one, a relationship that had been heading somewhere. Leo knew her, inside, where she rarely let many people in.

God, why did You rip away what was the desire of my heart?

She tilted her head back and watched puffy clouds drift across the blue sky. For the first time in over a year, she felt a sense of peace settle inside.

"What's wrong? You're frowning."

A cold soda appeared at her elbow. Rae looked up from her laptop. James had begun to join her most afternoons on the patio, and while she would not admit it to Lace, she had begun to look forward to his company.

"I think I need to rewrite chapter eighteen."

"Rae, the story is fine." He'd been up until 2:00 a.m. reading the manuscript. It was more than fine, it was wonderful. She just needed the courage to finish it.

"I think it's slow."

He pulled over a chair. "Give me the printout. Let me see."

She shifted the book holding down the manuscript pages and gave him the last four chapters. She gratefully drank the soda as she watched him read.

It was odd, how far their relationship had come in five days. She'd never expected to be so comfortable around him. She'd relaxed, and he'd turned into a very good friend.

"Read it again without page 314, I bet that's what you're sensing is wrong."

She paged back and forth in the on-line text. "That's it. It's too technical."

He picked up his own drink. "I want an autographed copy when it's published."

"James, it may never get finished, let alone find a publisher."

He smiled. "You'll finish it. You've got, what, another five hundred pages to go?"

She laughed. "Trust me to choose a big story to tell."

"I *like* the fact you think big."

She blinked. Smiled. "The kids catching any fish?"

"Emily's got six and Dave's only caught two. Emily's decided it is time to start giving him pointers, he's letting the team down."

Rae laughed. "How are Lace and Tom doing?"

"Scheming. They disappeared about an hour ago for what Tom called a 'super-duper' spot."

"That sounds like Tom. Got the time? Patricia asked to be woke up at four."

He glanced at his watch. "She's got another half hour."

"She's pregnant, isn't she?"

James grinned. "I sure think so. She was eating pickles for breakfast this morning."

He leaned back in his chair to pick up the book on the lounge chair that Rae had been reading that morning. Richard Foster's book on prayer. He liked her reading selection. "Is this one good?"

"Very."

"Bookstores and hot fudge sundaes were the two things I missed most about the States."

"I don't imagine the vanilla ice cream in Africa is the same as a Dairy Queen here."

"Didn't even come close. Want to ride to town with me to find some good ice cream?"

His offer caught her off guard.

Interesting . . . she looked like a doe caught in a car's headlights. "I promised Tom a banana split for having thrown a perfect spiral," he said gently. He'd just walked into something that caused her pain and he had no idea what it was.

"I think I'll pass."

There was the clatter of feet and the sound of laughter from the front porch. James squeezed her shoulder gently before walking inside to meet the fishing champs.

Several hours later, James carefully set the sack he held down on the kitchen counter. He flexed his wrist which had threatened to drop the package. The rest was helping, but he had such a long way to go before his body recovered. The only thing predictable was the pain. He would be so grateful to be able to do normal tasks like carry in the groceries without having to think about them first. Tom had disappeared down to the pavilion.

"Thank you, James," his sister said, walking in behind him. "I didn't mean to leave you with the groceries to carry in."

"It was three bags, Patricia," he said ruefully; the pain made it feel like thirty. "How's Emily's hand?"

"It's barely a scratch. A Band-Aid fixed it." She started putting away the groceries. "Since we've got cornmeal, should I deep-fry the fish as well as make hush puppies?"

"Most of the fish are bluegills — they are going to dress as popcorn pieces, so I would plan to deep-fry them. Do we have some newspaper we can use?"

"Under the sink, there's a stash just for cleaning fish."

James found them. "Thanks."

He glanced around as he left the cabin, then walked down to join Dave and Lace and the kids where they were preparing to clean the fish they had caught that afternoon. Rae was nowhere in sight.

It bothered him that he'd upset her with his earlier invitation to get ice cream. He had unintentionally touched a raw memory, and he needed to know that she was okay.

She'd been disappearing occasionally, taking some long walks. Hopefully, that was where she had headed this time.

She was getting her endurance back; she had made it to the top of the trail without being so out of breath she felt ready to collapse. Rae settled on the big rock that made a comfortable perch from which she could see most of the sandy stretch of beach. She had forty minutes before dinner, and had decided to take advantage of the time. She thought best when she hiked.

James's invitation had touched a raw nerve. There was no way he could have known Leo had taken her to that Dairy Queen the last summer they'd spent here. It bothered her that a simple question could throw her so badly.

She knew one reason the pain was lingering.

They would have had a child by now.

She wanted children. Deep inside, being a mother was part of who she wanted to be. She and Leo had talked at some length about having children, how they would restructure the business to let her work from home. She had been looking forward to having children almost as much as she had been looking forward to being married. She liked being single, but for a season in her life, not forever. She had been looking forward to his proposal. Learning he had been carrying the ring with him the night he had died had nearly broken her heart. It had simply been another indication of how unfairly life had treated her. She had been so close to the life she wanted, longed to have. It wasn't fair that it had been wrenched away from her.

The dream of having children was growing more distant.

She had lost so much of her life when Leo died.

It was so hard to keep letting go of pieces of her life. She propped her chin on her hand, rubbed her eyes. She liked to think, to plan, to look at the future. At times like this, she wanted to curse that part of her nature.

She had her work left, her book. Dave and Lace. An indefinite time of still being single.

The passion to earn money for her clients had disappeared during the last year. Two years ago the business had been something she had been willing to pour her life into, she had valued its success. Since Leo's death, the work had lost its compelling fascination. She was still good at it. She was even learning how to do Leo's job with reasonable skill. But it worried her that her heart wasn't in it, that her drive was gone. She had thought the vacation would help her be prepared to go back to work strong and focused and full of energy. Instead, the vacation was only contrasting how strongly she really didn't want to go back.

She was going to have to make some changes. She knew that. There were no margins left in her life, no time left in her schedule. It had been good and necessary in the past year to be so overwhelmingly busy, but she knew she could not continue in that mode another year.

There had to be a partner she would be comfortable working with, someone who could take Leo's place. She had been looking for a year to find someone who was a good trader, who had a track record to match Leo's. She wasn't having much luck. It was time to find someone who could replace her function, be the primary analyst, so she could consider moving permanently to Leo's trading position. It made her slightly sick to think about it, but the reality was, she couldn't carry both jobs indefinitely.

She tugged the notebook out of her pocket, looked again at the list she had been writing. So many components of the job had fallen behind due to lack of time. They weren't visible yet, but in another six months they would be. She had to hire a trader soon to free up her time to do the analysis. Every time she looked at the list of work to be done, Rae knew the decision had to be made.

The decision would have been made in the past over a cup of coffee and a stolen few minutes in Leo's office. It would have been decided and acted upon in a day. She hated running the business alone. The risks had been shared in the past, the decisions balanced by two opinions and two points of view.

She needed to accept and go on, build a life she would enjoy living.

It was a difficult proposition.

She didn't want the life she had.

She wanted the life she had lost.

"What's wrong?" Lace dropped down beside James on the steps. He gestured toward the campfire they had built down by the pavilion.

"Rae. She's restless tonight."

She had also been avoiding him all evening. He watched her get up from where she had been sitting, studying the fire, and pace down to the lake again. He hadn't meant to stir up her pain, and it was obvious that he had. She had looked strained when she came back from her walk, tired, and the sadness had been back in her eyes. He hated seeing it.

"How close were they, Lace?"

"Rae and Leo?"

James nodded.

"That last year, you would swear they were able to read each other's thoughts."

Lace pushed her hands into the pockets of her jacket. "Leo lived life with intensity. That's what drew people to him. He had the energy and boldness and courage to switch directions on a dime, take big risks. Rae was the perfect fit for him. She has the focus and depth and thirst for details necessary to break apart the problems, quantify them and see a way to make his vision happen."

James, watching Lace, saw deep concern etched in her face. "She hasn't been the same since Leo died. The sparkle that use to be inside when she talked about work is gone. They fed off each other, and she's lost without him. I think she's found the business was Leo's dream, one she had borrowed, and now that Leo's gone, she's trying to learn to do what he did naturally — take risks — and she's scared to death. She's not designed to take risks, it's not in her personality. To compensate, she's working hours that will put her into an early grave. About the only time I see glimpses of the old

Rae is when she's working on her book."

For the first time, James was starting to understand some of the complexity in the lady he had met. "She's using work to cope with the grief. That's not unusual, Lace."

"She's at the office at 5:00 a.m., doesn't leave until 7:00 sometimes 8:00 p.m. She makes Dave and me look like loafers. We haven't been able to shake her out of that routine."

"How much money is she managing?"

"About twenty-five million for thirty clients," Lace replied. "It could be seventy million if she said yes to even half the offers she gets."

Rae was driven by her own internal standards of excellence. Watching her with her book had shown James that. Add that kind of money to the equation, it was no wonder she was responding in the way she was. "She's good at what she does."

"Rae and Leo were the only money managers in the Midwest to have beaten the S&P 500 every year for the last seven years. Rae did it again on her own last year. She's on track to do it again this year. She's good. But her heart's not in it, James, not like it used to be."

"It would be a big risk to sell the business, walk away, Lace. You said yourself she's not going to easily take that kind of risk."

Their serious conversation was broken up by a shout of laughter from the pier.

"Dave just threw Rae into the lake," Emily told them, racing past. "She really needs my towel."

Lace got to her feet. "Excuse me, James. On behalf of my out-of-commission, best friend, Rae, I'm going to go help Dave join her."

"He's crazy to take both of you on."

"That's why we love him," Lace replied with a grin. "Keep what I said to yourself, okay? Rae's opinion about her work is different than mine."

"I will. The background helps, Lace."

She nodded, looked down at the group by the pier. "Mind if I borrow your flashlight?"

He handed it to her. "Just don't hit him with it."

She grinned. "I'm more refined than that. I think I'll suggest a late-night boat ride and let him swim back to shore."

The cabin was quiet, except for the sounds of the night drifting in — the soft sounds of rustling leaves, the distant call of an owl.

James had long since given up on trying to sleep. He lay in bed listening to the night, thinking, working out construction plans for the clinics he was going to build in Zaire.

He had loved the past weeks in the States with his family, his friends, but his heart was in Africa with the work that needed to be done. It was comforting to be able to focus on that and lay his plans. He would be able to hit the ground running when he got back in late August. They should have the first of the four clinics built and equipped by early November, the next one by the end of the year.

He needed to see about getting the equipment for the clinic expedited while he was in the States. A face-to-face meeting would ensure the urgency was understood.

He moved to shift the quilt and felt a familiar hot pain course through his elbow. He frowned, annoyed.

He had stopped asking God to heal him. He understood his Scripture, he understood the power of persistent prayer. He also understood the reality that nothing was going to stop God's plans from moving forward, not lack of money, not lack of building materials, not lack of government signatures, not lack of physical health for him. God knew what he needed and by when. James had stopped worrying about it. He had seen too many miracles in the last six years as God brought all the right pieces together for him to even worry about this need.

It would be nice, however, when he didn't have to fight this pain every time he moved.

He was on a vacation. He hadn't had one in six years. He was going to enjoy it and let tomorrow take care of itself. As long as the vacation was temporary.

This was nice, but it wasn't his dream.

He wanted to be back in Africa.

The sound of running water made him tilt his head to the side on the pillow, listen more closely to the sounds from inside the cabin. Someone was up.

He listened for the light steps of Emily or Tom to come back down the hall but heard nothing. Someone else was up at 3:00 a.m.? He had been the one to lock the cabin, set the dampers on the fireplace, turn off the lights at midnight. Everyone else had already turned in.

Not concerned, but curious, and wide awake anyway, James dressed in his sweatshirt and jeans.

Rae was curled up on the couch in black sweats, a book in her lap, a drink beside her on the table.

"Care for some company?"

She looked up, surprised. "Come on in, I

didn't realize you were still up."

"I could say the same thing about you."

"Catnap. It's really annoying to wake up at 3:00 a.m., wide awake. Normally I would find a financial report to read, but the cabin doesn't run to anything that dry. No use waking up Lace with my restless turning."

James settled into the chair opposite her. "What did you find?"

She glanced at the spine of the book. "*Biomechanics of the Human Hand.*"

"I'd say that qualifies as light reading," James replied, tongue-in-cheek.

"Actually, it's quite good. Some of their math is wrong, however. I spent twenty minutes looking at their torque calculations because I didn't understand their answer, only to realize they made a mistake in their math. It makes sense now."

"Let me guess, you took engineering classes as electives."

She grinned. "Doesn't everyone?"

"No," he replied, chuckling.

It was a nice time to talk, the dead of the night, no hurry to give a fast answer, no reason to break the silence until a new question occurred. Rae asked about the work in Africa, and James relaxed, enjoying the chance to talk about it.

He asked her about work, and while she

hesitated to answer at first, she was open and frank in what she said. He had heard Dave and Lace talking, had his conversation with Lace to go on. He knew how hard the past year had been on her. He avoided asking about Leo and she never volunteered his name.

Even so, he learned a lot, both about business and about Rae.

"What are the critical few pieces of information that drive your decisions? The day-to-day trading trends? The company earnings reports? The industry segment? The overall economy?"

"Most of the planning I do is around the company's ability to increase market share. That's the critical factor for knowing which companies I want to recommend. The right price to buy is driven by an analysis of the books and the style of management — are they aggressive in growing the business or conservative? How well do they use the assets they have? A company with small reserves but a willingness to use them is invariably a better buy than a company with large reserves that passes up opportunities. When to sell is a crap shoot — I know the fundamentals, but it's hard to judge how far the market will take a stock that is rising beyond what its fundamentals can support.

Invariably, I sell too soon."

He listened to her, observed her and he realized something. Rae on her own turf, in her domain of expertise, was decisive, clear and confident. She loved the analysis, being able to make the call with confidence, having the facts to make the right decision. Her job perfectly matched her talents and gifts. She was known as one of the best at what she did because she was one of the best — others could only imitate what came to her intuitively, naturally, by instinct.

"No, a red card does not mean it is a diamond," Rae informed Dave, picking up the cards, overriding his appeal that he had won the hand with a trump card. "A bluff only works if the other person buys it."

"Face it, Dave, I can read you like an open book. I knew you didn't have it," Lace told him, smirking.

"Lace, you can't be successful all night," Dave replied, tossing a piece of popcorn at her.

James had figured the bridge game would be a serious event. He should have known better.

The ladies were killing them.

Rae had managed to bluff and win two

hands and Lace had just nailed the ladies' second hand.

Tom, acting as Lace's partner, finished scoring the hand. "Lace, you really are good."

"Thank you, Tom," Lace said, pleased.

Rae shuffled the cards with the ease of someone who had handled a deck of cards for years. "Want to cut?" she offered Dave.

He offered the cards to Emily, sitting beside him.

The little girl grinned.

Rae dealt the cards, a flip of her wrist landing the cards directly in front of each person at the table. "Your bid," she told James.

"Two clubs."

Dave and Lace ended up going head to head again, both holding the last of the trump cards.

Dave laid down the three of hearts. "Sorry, honey. You've been got."

Lace laid down her last card with a smile. "You need to count better, friend." The five of hearts.

Rae burst out laughing at Dave's expression.

"Next year we're going to play Monopoly," Dave told Lace, as Rae collected the cards.

"I would love to be your landlord," Lace replied, grinning.

"Rae, mind some company?" James asked quietly, stopping at the bottom steps to the pavilion. The bridge game had concluded a little over an hour ago. He had left Dave and Lace haggling in the kitchen over the best way to reheat spaghetti left over from dinner, and come out to walk along the lake before turning in for the night. He had thought Rae had already gone to bed, instead he found her sitting alone in the pavilion, looking at the water.

Tomorrow they would be packing up and heading home.

"Come on up," she replied, her voice quiet.

He touched her shoulder as he reached the bench.

She was cold.

He slipped off his jacket and draped it over her shoulders.

"Thanks." She buried her hands into the warmth, one last shiver shaking her frame.

"You should have come back to the cabin for a jacket."

"I didn't realize I was this cold."

James settled on the bench beside her, pushed his hands into the pockets of his jeans. The water was tranquil tonight, the moonlight reflecting off its surface, dancing around. A multitude of stars were out. Nights in Africa had been like this — panoramic in their display.

"What's wrong?" he asked quietly. She didn't disappear in the middle of the night without something driving her actions.

She eventually sighed. "I don't want the vacation to end."

He turned to look at her. There was so much sadness in her voice. "Why, Rae?" he asked gently.

"I've enjoyed the last several days working on the book. I don't want to give it up." She leaned back, looked up at the stars, a pensive look on her face. "It's simple to say I'll make time to write when I get home, but the reality is, there won't be time. There is so much work to do, it's overwhelming."

"You're tired." Tired of the pace of life, tired of the weight, tired of carrying the responsibility, tired of being alone. . . . How well he understood tired.

She sighed. "In three days, this will all be only a distant memory. I'll be living on adrenaline again, going from one crisis to another."

"Rae, you can change it. The schedule is reflecting your choices."

"I have a responsibility to my clients to see that the job is done well. I've been looking for someone to step in and help manage the business, looking hard, but it just hasn't happened yet."

He knew what it felt like to be the one carrying the responsibility to make sure a situation worked out. You did whatever had to be done, it was that simple. The early days in business with Kevin, most of the last six years in Africa . . . a commitment was kept, even if it meant long hours and a lot of lost sleep. But the doctors had been pretty frank — they didn't think his symptoms would be as severe had he not been pushing himself so hard for so long.

"I've watched you this week. You're one of the best planners I have ever met. You can manage the business until you find someone. Just don't let yourself get overwhelmed. Set some limits, do what you can and walk away from it," he advised, wishing he had learned to heed his own advice at some point in his past.

"I've never learned how to walk away and really leave my work at the office. It's been haunting my sleep the last few months," she admitted quietly. "I don't want to go back to that, James. It's not worth it."

How he wished he could take away the

burden or make it easier to carry. Words were such a limited help.

He thought about how dramatically the past five months had changed him. He had that to offer, the reality of what it was to know the tasks exceeded the resources to meet them. "Rae, I've had to learn the hard way that you have to accept and live with the limits you are dealt. You're going to have to set limits around how much energy you can pour into work, how much stress you can carry. When you reach your limits, walk away. The world won't stop functioning if you take twelve hours for yourself."

"No, I might only lose my client's shirt."

He smiled. "Somehow, from what I hear, I doubt that is very likely. You've got to learn, Rae, that taking a break is just as legitimate a use of your time as continuing to work."

She sighed. "I feel guilty when I leave a job unfinished."

How well James understood that guilt. "Believe me, I feel the same way. Limits are never easy, but Rae, in the long run, they prove their worth. Maybe I'm fortunate with this illness to have at least learned that. My body no longer allows me to exceed my limits. It forces me to stop and rest. I wish it would do it in a somewhat less drastic fashion — the pain and fatigue are intense. But it's made me learn to set priorities for what I will use my energy to do."

"It's come down to prioritizing good versus good. I can either ensure the day-to-day decisions are right and on time and risk sacrificing the big picture, or I can focus on the future analysis and risk the day-to-day trading. It's a no-win situation," Rae said.

James stopped his train of thought, realizing something. "Rae, do you like your job?"

She was surprised by the question. Surprised enough to stop and think about it before she tried to answer it. When she did, her answer seemed to surprise her. "I want time to work on the book. I want time to spend with friends. I want the job, but not at the expense of those two needs." She smiled. "Ambivalence. I never thought I would feel that about work. In the past, it's been the passion and driving goal of my life. I don't know when it disappeared."

"Leo's death," James said softly.

She thought about it. "No. It changed before that. The day I said yes to going out with Leo. What I wanted in my life changed. I'm good at the job, I just don't want it to be the only thing in my life anymore. I shifted gears inside to planning for a marriage and a family."

She sighed. "I don't know what I want anymore." She considered that statement for a moment. "Yes I do. I want Leo back."

He liked her honesty, her ability to be frank. "It's tough to adjust when you know what you want isn't going to happen," he commented, knowing some of what it felt like from his own frustration with this medical furlough. "Figure out a way to put time into your schedule to write, to spend time with Lace. Reevaluate what you think about work when you've fixed those problems," he suggested.

She really did love her job. He was convinced of that. She just needed it to be her job again, instead of her life. Rae was tired, but the love of the job was still there, buried under the weight of the responsibility she was carrying.

"I've been trying to think about ways to make my time during the day less fragmented — the trading is a reactive job, something I didn't have to deal with before. That's what's killing my ability to do the analysis work. There has to be a way to improve the situation."

James was grateful to hear some of the tension had left her voice. "You'll find it, Rae. Think of it as a puzzle to solve."

She laughed. "A puzzle called Rae's Day on the Job. That's what it is, too, a problem to be analyzed and solved. It can't continue as it currently is."

"I hate to be the one to suggest this, but it is getting late. We had probably better turn in for the night."

She had yawned twice and her face was showing her weariness. She needed to be in bed.

Rae nodded, pushing herself away from the bench. "Thanks for being willing to talk work, James. I know it's not the most interesting subject."

He smiled. "Oh, I don't know. It's a good chunk of your life right now. I'm interested."

"Why?"

"Just because," James replied, dropping his arm around her shoulders as they walked back to the cabin.

He stepped back as they entered the back door, let her precede him. Patricia had put the kids to bed a while ago. Dave and Lace had turned in; the cabin was quiet. "I'll see you in the morning, Rae. Sleep well."

He was surprised by her attempt to contain a smile. "You, too, James. Good night," she said softly.

It was as he was climbing under his covers

that James realized he'd been truly enfolded into this close-knit family of friends.

They had short-sheeted his bed.

Chapter Five

Fifty laps. James touched the wall, breathing hard, and let the water lap around him as he let his body relax. His endurance was back. His body ached, not with pain, but with the exertion of a good workout.

Smiling, pleased, he swam at a leisurely pace to the ladder.

He was over the worst of the symptoms.

Eight weeks of a lot of sleep, a lot of medicine, and careful exercise had paid off. His joints no longer ached.

He had already talked his next step over with Kevin. He thought his body was ready to tackle a building project again. It was time to know. Three weeks working on a house with Kevin would tell him if he was right.

The smell of chlorine was strong in the air as James crossed the tile deck to the chair where he had left his towel and locker key. The health club was surprisingly empty for a Thursday afternoon. A glance at the wall clock showed he had just enough time for ten minutes in the whirlpool followed by a quick shower before he needed to leave to pick up Dave.

Rae was bowling in the finals tonight.

She was still too busy to suit any of them, but James had watched her eyes begin to smile again, knew Rae was adjusting, finding a balance between her life and her work.

He'd become one of the group.

His initiation had been one short-sheeted bed. He still had no idea which one of them had done it, but they had all obviously known about it.

In the six weeks since, he had come to profoundly appreciate their offer of friendship.

He was part of the group.

He'd never experienced anything like it, a camaraderie coupled with loyalty that went so deep as to be nearly unbreakable. He had begun to realize the significance of it the day Dave flew back on a chartered flight from San Diego during a trial to be at an awards banquet where Lace was speaking, and from the awards banquet went back to the airport for a return trip in the middle of the night. It was Rae networking her contacts to donate the medical equipment he would need for the clinics then pulling more strings to get even the shipping costs donated. It was Lace putting in an all-nighter with Dave to prepare a court defense, then getting on a plane herself to make a major presentation the next day. It was Friday night dinners at Dave's place, movies at Lace's, basketball games as Rae's. It was a network of names and contacts and favors that they used freely to solve problems for each other, from getting plane tickets on a moment's notice to getting phone calls to the top executive of a corporation put through. It was inconceivable amounts of cash flowing from one individual or another to needs the group spotted. It was a common "what I have is yours" use of their time, resources and talents. Cementing it all together was a lot of laughter.

They were friends.

They had chosen him to be one of them.

As the weeks went by, he had grown to appreciate how big a blessing God had dropped in his life.

He had become their expert advisor on cars, construction, real estate, large organization management, and, somehow, their elected chief arbitrator of decisions. There would be options on the table for what to do, where to go, whom to call, priorities to set. And when he finally stated what he thought, they would go that way. He had finally understood a few weeks back that they were doing it intentionally. They wanted him to be part of the team, not a newcomer.

He was going to miss them when Africa put him half a world away.

Six weeks, and he would be standing on scrubland, putting a clinic together where there was only a dream and a need.

He had a feeling that the three of them had simply decided they were going to extend their network around the globe to follow him. Dave had been adding contacts in the State Department to his Rolodex; Lace had already put her international banking contacts at his disposal; Rae, through the foundation money she managed, was already picking his brain for details about the type of doctors he needed to staff the clinics.

They were being friends.

They hadn't been able to solve his medical problems, but they had literally put in his hand access to one of the best health clubs in the area, the private cards of the best doctors in the city, even season tickets to the White Sox games.

There were times he marveled at the blessings God chose to give. This group of friends could have only been conceived and put together by the hand of God.

"Anything else, Janet?" Rae asked, pausing on her way back from a telephone conference with Gary in Seattle and Mike in Houston.

Her secretary glanced down her running list. "Mark said he would fax the corporate resolutions over tonight, Linda had a question on the tax distribution from March — I had the information she needed so I faxed it to her — I need a decision on when you would like to meet with Quinn Scott, and Bob Hamilton wants to have lunch next week to follow up on your proposal."

Rae felt like doing a dance, but settled for a significant smile. "Accept any day next week that Bob Hamilton has available — I'll call and apologize to whomever you have to bump from my schedule. Remind me to send Dave a thank-you. Pencil Quinn in for either late Tuesday or Wednesday afternoon next week."

Janet added the information to her list. "I'll leave you a confirmation message on your voice mail and update the board with what I can arrange. That looks like it."

"Wonderful. Thanks, Janet."

Rae was going to be able to leave the

office by 6:00 p.m. The changes made in the past six weeks had finally begun to pay off.

She entered the trading room for one last review of the day's events. She had the place to herself, a rare occurrence.

Mr. Potato Head was smiling.

Rae grinned and tipped his pipe down. Leo's toys still dotted the room. She'd never had the heart to remove them. This was still his domain, even today. Besides, she liked his toys, they each had a story to tell that made her smile.

It was a spacious room made crowded by the volume of equipment. She glanced at the news feeds, three televisions monitoring CNN, the financial channel and the news channel, all three taped for playback in case of breaking news, then at the bank of stock price monitors. Leo had written the software driving the price monitors. One monitor showed prices and movements for all the stocks they owned, another monitor showed prices and movements for stocks on their watch list, and the last monitor showed prices and volumes in the market as a whole.

Scott was breaking down the stocks that had dropped or jumped up during the day, would give his recommendations by voice mail tonight; she would do her own analysis of the data in the morning in light of his recommendations and make some decisions.

Rae settled down in the captain's chair and tipped back, sipping the cup of coffee she had brought with her as she watched the terminals on the trends desk flip through the daily, monthly and yearly graphs for each stock they owned. She paused the progression of the graphs occasionally, adding a few of them to her work list for the morning. On the whole she was satisfied with what she saw.

A touch of a key flipped the display to client portfolios. Rae took her time reviewing the thirty-two screens, looking at the effects the day's markets had had on her clients' portfolios.

It had been a good day overall.

All the information she was looking at was available in her own office, but she had decided after coming back from vacation that it would be a strategic move to separate the analysis and planning work she did from the trading work she also directed.

After six weeks, her office felt like a haven again. She had to worry about instant decisions and responding to events when she was here in the war room; outside of this room, she could back off to her more natural planning mode. It had been a good compromise.

Hiring two more excellent secretaries and thinking through carefully what data she needed to see each morning had let her focus that critical first forty minutes of her day. At Lace's insistence, she now had breakfast being delivered for everyone in the office at 7:00 a.m. Her appetite was still nonexistent, but Janet was keeping a watch on her, showing up with a plate of food if she forgot to stop working to eat. Rae was pretty sure the dozen roses on the corner of Janet's desk were from Dave. Trust her friends to have a spy in her office.

A glance at the middle clock on the wall, the one set for Central Standard Time, showed ten minutes before six. It was time to get moving. She needed to swing by Lace's condo and pick up Dave's leather jacket on the way to the bowling alley. How Dave's most cherished possession had ended up at Lace's place in July was a mystery Rae intended to solve before the night was out.

Lace had been in Canada for a conference, it could have conceivably been cool enough she would need a jacket, but Dave's leather jacket? It wasn't fashionable. And Dave didn't exactly just hand that jacket out. Letting a lady wear that jacket was Dave's equivalent of giving a class ring.

"Nail it, Rae."

She stopped the swing, the loud call coming just as she began to step forward, the momentum spinning her around. "Would my cheering section please quit interrupting my concentration?" she demanded, amused.

"Why? You bowl better when we interrupt you," Dave said.

"Your only strikes came with our help," Lace confirmed, her patent leather shoes resting on the back of the chair in front of the bench. She was shelling peanuts. She looked about sixteen with the outfit she had on — the poodle skirt was vintage sixties if it was a day, the bubble gum had to be interfering with the peanuts, and her hair was in two ponytails. Two. It was carrying cheerleading beyond the call of duty. It did explain the leather jacket.

"How many strikes is that?"

"Two," James added cheerfully from his seat as acting scoring secretary.

She scowled at him. She was having a rotten game.

"Try to behave, you're embarrassing my team."

"They're okay, Rae," the rest of her bench chimed in. Dave tipped his can of soda in thank-you for the support. He had bought the first round of soft drinks for the entire league. He was everyone's pal tonight.

Rae reset her position, considered what Leo would have done in this situation, and laid a blistering twist on the release, crossing her ball over the fifth board. She watched it flair out to the second board, cross the second set of diamonds and promptly hook into a pocket with a vicious pop.

"All right, Rae!"

She walked back to the bench, smiling.

She slapped hands with her teammates and picked up the towel she had tossed on her seat.

"You're a pretty good player, aren't you?" James leaned forward across the back of the seat to whisper.

"Sort of," Rae whispered back. "We promised the league we would make the games competitive this year."

"So, where are we going from here?"

It was late, and the foursome paused in the parking lot to consider Dave's question.

Dave had his arm draped around Lace's shoulders. James could understand why he didn't want the evening to end. He didn't particularly want to see the evening end, either.

Rae paused beside him as they considered what they would do, shifting her bag holding two bowling balls to her other hand. He had offered to carry it for her, but she had declined with a smile and a soft thanks. He hadn't made an issue of it. The symptoms were gone, but she was still being cautious. Either that, or she didn't want his help. He preferred to think she was still being careful of his wrists. The first time at the bowling alley, weeks ago, he had picked up a bowling ball and the pain in his wrist had made him nearly gasp in pain. Tonight, he bet he could bowl a game and not feel even a twinge.

"James, will a late night be a problem?" Rae asked him in an undertone, confirming his suspicions of what she was thinking.

He appreciated the question, but he really was okay now. "No."

"We could go to Avanti's for a pizza," she suggested to the group.

"Great idea. They have the best garlic bread sticks," Lace commented.

"Garlic? Lace . . ." Dave began to protest.

Lace slipped out from under his arm. "Don't go making assumptions, Dave. I'll ride with Rae and we'll meet you two there."

Dave sighed. "Sure."

James hid his smile, aware, as was Rae, how Lace and Dave were skirting around actually dating. "Come on Dave, ride with me and give me directions. I'll bring you back here to pick up your car."

They walked across the parking lot to the car Kevin had loaned him, listening to the laughter of the ladies as they walked in the other direction to Rae's Lexus.

James unlocked the car, catching sight of Dave's expression as he turned to watch them. "She does like you, you know."

"I thought getting a kiss when I was sixteen was a big deal," Dave commented. "It's nothing like trying to get one from Lace. I've never met a lady with more contrary signals in my life."

"She doesn't want to mess up a friendship."

"No, it's not that. Rae was like that. I think Lace just likes to be contrary. I made the mistake of asking her out only after I found out she was dating some tax attorney. She's miffed at me."

James smiled. "She looked really miffed tonight."

Dave gave him directions to the restaurant. He smiled. "She does make nice company. But James, I swear, she's going to

115

have me going in circles for months before she says yes."

"So, ask her to something you know she can't refuse. She's into art in a big way isn't she?"

"Impressionists."

"Find a showing she would love to see, make it hard for her to turn you down," James suggested.

"That's a good idea."

James turned east on Hallwood street, easily keeping Rae's Lexus in view up ahead.

"What's Rae like to do?" he asked casually — too casually — a few minutes later. He had a few weeks before he left the country; he wouldn't mind spending some of that time with Rae. He enjoyed her company.

Dave laughed. "Not aiming low, are you?" He thought for a moment. "Rae? I guess I would put bookstores at the top of her list, pet stores, charity auctions, medical conferences. Any conference related to work — financial planning, taxes, stock selection. She's always been pretty hard to pin down."

"Does she dance?"

Dave looked troubled. "I would recommend that you stay away from it. Leo was trying to teach her."

Dave pointed out the restaurant. "They were two days away from being engaged, James. She's still dealing with a lot of big issues. I'm not saying don't pursue it, but I would move cautiously if I were you."

Engaged.

Lace hadn't told him that.

James slid out of the booth as the ladies came to join them, allowed Rae to slip back into her seat. She was sitting beside him in the booth.

It had been a laughter-filled last thirty minutes. Rae was still riding high with energy, her team having won the competition, and Dave was in usual form tonight, keeping them laughing at his stories. James was finding it hard to join in. He kept considering the implications of what Dave had said.

Engaged.

There was a lot of pain to process when you lost someone you loved. It may have been almost two years, but when he looked at Rae, he knew she had a long way to go before she had processed all the grief. The implications of how her life had changed — the work pressure, the added weight of responsibility, were still fundamentally affecting her life.

How well he could remember the first time he met her, how deep the grief had been in her eyes. Now, after weeks around her, he was catching glimpses of Rae without that pain; moments when the glimmer of laughter would reach her eyes, moments when her smile would cause her eyes to twinkle. As a friend, he wanted to see that healing continue. He wanted to help in any way he could. As a man, he wanted her to be able to move on from the past.

He liked her.

It was a pretty profound emotion, because he wanted it to be more than a casual friendship.

He knew the reality. He was returning to Africa in six weeks. He had an obligation and commitment there to finish what he had begun, and the need was there, but the part of him that looked at the cost of that commitment was chalking up Rae as one of the steeper costs he was going to be paying.

Before he went back to Africa, he would like to see the smile in her eyes there all the time.

He wouldn't mind spending more time with her before he went back overseas, simply because he enjoyed listening to her and being with her. But he no longer could treat her past as a casual fact. It was big and powerful, and to be a friend he had to at least appreciate what that past meant to her. Until tonight, he really hadn't understood.

It made the idea of asking her out take on a whole new implication.

She hadn't been on a date since Leo passed away. He ought to have at least realized that before he popped off a casual question. No wonder his suggestion of going into town to get ice cream had startled her.

She hadn't been prepared to hear such a casual offer.

He would know better in the future.

He smiled as he listened to Rae debate Dave over the merits of the latest tax cap proposal for the county, Lace interrupting occasionally to add her concerns. The three of them had a passion for politics and legislation that made him wonder why none of them had ever gone into politics. The debate came down to point of interpretation and all three of them looked at him.

He grinned as he picked up his soda. "Sorry, I can't even give an opinion."

"We've got to stop doing local politics," Lace apologized, pushing her plate to the side.

"Who wants the last two pieces of pizza?" Between the four of them, a large Canadian bacon pizza had nearly disappeared.

"Rae," he and Dave said at the same time.

Rae rolled her eyes. "I don't need to gain that much."

"A bird has been eating more than you have. Take it for lunch tomorrow," Dave insisted.

Rae conceded because she was outvoted. James leaned back in the bench and watched Rae, a smile on his face because she was beside him and because occasionally she would turn to ask him a question in a low voice so the other two wouldn't hear and her eyes would be sparkling. She had chosen him, since Dave and Lace were skirting around actually dating each other, to be the one she would turn to when she needed a partner. She sent him to get her soda, asked him to find the hot pepper shaker for her. Little things that made him smile. She'd returned the favor by announcing Dave was buying the pizza. Dave had groaned and protested and she'd just looked at him, prompting laughter around the table when Dave didn't say another word.

Rae was happy tonight and he didn't want the night to end.

She needed more breaks like this. He'd been thinking about it as they sat and talked tonight. He had one option up his sleeve, something he thought might get a yes from her even though everything he had seen so far said she was comfortable in the group of friends, but not beyond that group. Puppies were a hard date to turn down.

"Have a nice night?"

His mom was still up, seated in the recliner in the family room, knitting, the late show just finishing, credits scrolling by on the screen. It was like walking back in time. So many times during his high school and college days he had come home and found her in just that chair, reading a book, watching a late show, occasionally sleeping. It was his dad's chair.

James leaned against the doorpost, tucked his hands in his pockets, smiled. "Real good, Mom."

For all the pain and trouble the bug he had picked up had caused, the fact that it gave him a few weeks back with family almost made it worthwhile. He was storing up memories of his mom and his sister and her family. He was going to miss them all.

"I'm glad." She set down the sweater she was making, then touched the remote to shut off the television. "I do love Cary Grant. He made such good movies."

His dog leveraged himself to his feet, came over to greet him. "Hi, boy." James stroked the dog's coat and he lazily leaned against James's jeans, loving the attention.

His mom picked up the bowl of orange peels beside the chair and the empty glass off the table. "Your dad and I watched that movie on our honeymoon." She touched the light switch. "There were a couple phone calls for you tonight. Jim Marshall called from Germany and Kevin called, said to tell you Monday was good on his schedule. I left the notes on the kitchen table."

"I bet Jim's got a new baby to announce. Heather was due about now," James remarked walking back to the kitchen to get the message.

"It would be his second?"

"Third. He's got a boy and girl." He confirmed the number was the one he remembered. "I've got a couple guys coming over tomorrow to help me rehang the garage door so it won't stick anymore. I'll be over at the kennels after that. Did your dog Margo have her puppies yet?"

"Not yet, but the vet says she's due anytime. Bobby said he would be sure to check on her tonight when he makes his rounds."

"I've got someone I think I'll invite over

122

to see them," James said casually.

His mom smiled, that smile she use to get when he said he was bringing a girl home with him to study.

"I'm leaving in six weeks, Mom."

His mom nodded, but her smile only got wider. "Six weeks is a long time. Rae will like the puppies. Lock up before you turn in?"

James knew he had said nothing about Rae recently, he'd seen her only as part of the group. He spent his time with Dave or Kevin or over at Patricia's. Trust his mom to figure out his interest before he did. . . .

"I'll lock up."

"It's good to have you back, James," Kevin said, handing him the second cup of coffee he was carrying.

It was the crack of dawn, dew was still on the cars and trucks, and they were looking at what was essentially a hardened pad of concrete. Not a piece of lumber had been laid for this house that was slated to be ready for the electrician and plumber in three weeks.

"Remember how to be a carpenter?"

James laughed. "I've forgotten more than you ever learned," he replied, drinking the coffee and looking over the blueprints spread out before them across two sawhorses. He was eager, impatient to get to work; he had always loved these initial few days, framing in a house and making it appear from nothing.

His devotions that morning had landed on Psalm 127. *Unless the Lord builds the house, those who build it labor in vain.* It was just like God to note the arrival of this day with the same expectation James felt.

It was nice to know this morning he was going to be helping God build a home.

"The rest of the crew should be arriving anytime. Find the chalk and let's get this house underway," Kevin said. "I've missed this, James. I've been stuck behind a desk too much the last couple of years."

"Have you sold this one yet?"

"A real nice couple from Georgia, moving with his job. They've got one little girl, about six years old."

The lumber for the frame had been delivered and rested on pallets on what would someday be a sodded backyard. James started hauling lumber. The first nail drove into the wood in two decisive blows of the hammer, making him smile and reach for the next nail.

He was back.

This was who he was.

A carpenter who made homes and clinics

rise where there was only a dream.

It felt good. Really, really good.

God, thanks. The prayer came from his heart. It was followed with another nail, pounded in with a smile. There was a day coming in heaven when he was going to get the Master Craftsman in a workshop to show him the things He had made when He was a carpenter. There was something uniquely satisfying with sharing the profession Jesus had chosen for thirty years. Jesus could have been a farmer or a fisherman, or a shopkeeper. He had chosen to be a carpenter. James could understand why.

Chapter Six

✝

"James, can you join us? We're at Rae's to-night," Dave asked.

Ten hours on the job studding in the kitchen had left him dripping in sweat and physically tired, a good tired that came after accomplishing a good job, but still ready for some downtime. He had been headed for a shower and a ball game when the phone had rung. His mom was out tonight with Patricia and the kids.

"What time, Dave? I'll be there."

It was Rae. Any other offer he would have declined. Going to Rae's put the request in a different league.

"Seven-thirty. Lace is coming out from the city."

"I'll be there."

"Great. Come hungry. I'm doing ribs on the grill."

James hung up the phone. Rae. He hadn't seen her for eight days. He had checked the nursery Sunday morning to find he had just missed her. Eight days was too long.

Margo had four gorgeous puppies, but James had decided a phone call was not the way to extend the invitation. He needed to do it in person, when he knew it was a favorable time and he would see her expression.

Tonight.

Ask Rae over for dinner and a trip to the kennel to see the puppies.

Add his mom to the picture. Dinner at his mom's kitchen table. That should be low-key enough to get a yes. Nothing threatening. It would get him a few hours of her company, that was the objective.

He went to take a shower, his fatigue easing with the plans for the night.

After four days of construction work with Kevin, his body was complaining about the physical exertion, but so far it was the aches and pains he would expect from having been sidelined for so many weeks. It wasn't the pain he had learned to dread, pain burning in his joints; it was the normal ache of muscles being used to do some heavy work.

He was relieved.

He had been more worried than he was willing to admit about how this first week of construction would go. He wasn't out of danger of a physical surprise yet, but every day that went by put him all the more closer to being able to return to Africa. He prayed for that every morning when he got up, every evening when he went to bed.

Africa.

It was work he did well. It was work that saved lives.

He was enjoying the comforts of a hot shower, a good meal and a soft bed while he had them. They would soon be memories. He had learned to enjoy good things while they were there. It was a cost of the mission field. He had accepted the cost once before, and he would accept it again.

There was a world in need, and he had the skills to meet it. To not go would be to deny the call God had placed on his heart.

Someday, there would be a payoff worth the sacrifice.

It was time to quit wishing for something else and enjoy what God had given now. Good friends. A wonderful lady. Ribs.

Dave was awesome with charcoal and a grill.

"Dave, did you need matches?" Rae shifted the casserole dish of scalloped potatoes to the top of the stove, careful to keep a firm grip on the hotpad. She had already burned her thumb once tonight.

"Got them, Rae. Were you able to find the long tongs?"

"Yes, but I need to wash them," Rae called out to the deck. "I'll have them for you in a minute."

She blew a strand of hair back from her eyes. Company was coming and she was a wreck. Still in her skirt and blouse from work, rumpled, hot, running late.

"Would you quit fussing over the food and go take a shower? It's just James and Lace," Dave said, joining her in the kitchen.

Exactly, Rae thought. She preferred James to see her with a semblance of her act together.

Dave laughed and took the pot holders. "Go. I can manage the kitchen."

She hugged him then deserted him, leaving him to try to put together the menu.

The shower was hot, the steam taking away the marks of the stressful day. It had been a day where she had been silently pleading by noon for God to send her some relief. The markets had been volatile, one of the computer feeds of data had gone down, and Janet had been called for jury duty.

Rae rapidly washed her hair.

God, we've talked about it so many times in the past six weeks. I'm glad You're using James to help pull me out of the grief, but God, just be-

129

tween You and me, this is getting embarrassing. He's a friend, he's going back to Africa in six weeks, and I'm acting like I've got a crush on him! I'm not cut out to be acting like I'm twenty again. I'm not ready to emotionally deal with a guy and a relationship again. So would you please ease this emotion and use tonight to help me back off?

Oh, and God, if I get a chance to talk to Lace alone tonight, help me find the right words to say. She's been quietly hoping for Dave's interest for three years. Now that he's asked, she needs the courage to say yes. I understand her fears, Dave has not exactly shown a desire to settle down in the past, but I've seen something different in him the past few weeks, and I want Lace to at least give him a chance. I think they were made for each other, Lord. They complement each other, and they've already got the commitment to each other as friends.

The silent prayer helped steady Rae's nerves. Ten minutes later, standing in front of her closet biting her bottom lip, she had to make a decision. She wanted comfortable and Lace would argue she should go for knockout. Rae hated waffling about clothes. She had no idea what she should wear. She finally chose a black knit top and a pair of pressed jeans. She added her mother's pearls. It was a compromise.

It took forever to get her hair to dry. When she finally clicked off the hair dryer, she could hear voices from downstairs. She glanced at the clock. Lace had made better time than she expected.

Rae hesitated, then reached over for the perfume bottle.

It was a night of friends over for a meal and a televised baseball game. She had to get over these nerves. She finally had to order herself to get downstairs and be the hostess.

James parked behind Lace's car in the drive. As he walked up the drive to the town house, he could hear laughter coming from the deck at the back.

Rae had a beautiful home. He let himself in, having concluded they were all outside. It was a comfortable place, nice furniture, beautiful paintings, restful because it was lived in. Rae had her mom's books — eight novels, prominently displayed in the living room. Her mail had been dropped in a basket on the kitchen bar, magazines tossed in a basket beside the couch.

There were books everywhere, on book-shelves in the living room, a stack on the hallway table to be returned to the library, a half-dozen more piled up on the floor at the end of the couch, most with a bookmark indicating where she had left off reading.

The first time he had seen her home, he had been impressed with how well it reflected her personality. It wasn't coordinated as a decorator would do it, but it was visually restful and functionally useful.

Rae was a lady who liked pictures, most of the shelves and a few of the tables had framed snapshots. Her family. Dave and Lace. Leo.

Rae had a picture of Leo on the shelf beside her mom's novels. It was a candid snapshot, obviously taken by either Lace or Dave, at the cabin where they had vacationed. Leo had been in the kitchen making waffles, Rae leaning against his back and reaching around to swipe a strawberry. The snapshot told James a lot. Leo had turned to say something to Rae, and the expression on his face as he looked at her had been unguarded. Leo had been in love with Rae. It was there in his face and his eyes.

He had been a good man.

Everything Dave and Lace said, everything Rae herself reflected, told him that.

The fact Rae had kept the snapshot, displayed it as she did, was a tribute to the fact the love had been returned.

The pictures of Rae with Leo, other pictures around, had given him a glimpse of a

Rae he had not met, one who was relaxed, happy, not yet touched by grief.

Her smile was returning, but it was a slow process.

God, are You sure an invitation is the right thing to do? I'm back to waffling again.

James followed the sound of laughter to the deck just in time to see Dave duck the spray of the water hose Lace was holding. She had obviously been trying to help with the flaring flames licking the charcoal and threatening to burn the ribs, but she hadn't been ready for the fact Rae had turned the valve on.

James bit back a laugh at the scene.

Lace meekly turned the hose over to a Dave who was now standing in wet shoes. "Sorry, David."

Dave wiped the water off his forearm, gave a long-suffering sigh. "You know, the first time I could write it off as an accident, but the third time? I swear you just like to get me soaked, Lace."

"Would some iced tea make it better?"

He tweaked a lock of her hair at the amusement in her voice. "Make it a soda with caffeine. I have a feeling I'm going to need it tonight."

The wind shifted and James got a smell of the cooking ribs. A day working on a house made a man hungry. He stepped out onto the deck.

"Hi, James." Rae walked onto the deck, pausing beside him.

She was beautiful tonight, her hair pulled back in a gold barrette, the length brushing her shoulders. The pearls were a sharp contrast to the black sweater. He didn't see her wear jewelry very often. "Hi, Rae. Looks like I got here just in time."

"Be glad you weren't here a few minutes earlier, you would have probably gotten doused as well."

She seemed a little uncertain around him, not meeting his glance. James wondered ruefully what was wrong. He wished she would relax around him like she did with Dave.

"James, can I get you a drink?" Lace asked.

Lace, as always, was dressed casually, yet looking like a fashion model. "A soft drink would be fine," he replied, returning her smile.

"I made my special sauce I was telling you about. You are going to like these ribs." James accepted the inevitable and went to join Dave.

James settled in with Dave, talking food, and looking around the yard, noting a few things that needed done. Rae didn't have enough time in her life to keep a yard landscaped, he knew that, but there was evidence that in the past she had tried.

The trellis with the grapevines needed to have a few slates added to bear the weight of the full vines. And her rosebushes were in full bloom, though a couple needed to be trimmed back.

He missed not having a house and yard to work on. Years before, when the business with Kevin had finally begun to turn a modest profit, he had bought an older two-story home near where Patricia currently lived and used his free time to fix it up. He had enjoyed the work, both inside and out in the yard. When he had sold the home the summer he went to Africa, it had been like parting with an old friend. He had made good money on the investment, but it had been a sacrifice, selling the place.

He was a man who liked having a home that showed the benefits of his labor. For six years on the mission field, he had accepted living in temporary housing, often staying with members of the local church, their hospitality appreciated and generous, but it was not the same as having a permanent home.

Dave had a restless, nomadic streak. James was different. He looked forward to the day the clinics were built and the job was done, coming back to the States to settle in one place, buy a house and use his labor to make it a nice home.

Lace returned with the soda he had requested.

Dave flipped the ribs over, added more barbecue sauce.

Ten minutes later, they settled around the table for dinner. Rae and Lace sat across from Dave and James.

Rae was quiet, but her smile was genuine, her laughter making her eyes twinkle. Although she was still avoiding catching his glance, he had a long evening to work on getting her attention.

Rae passed him the bread and he finally caught her eye. He smiled and it was tentative, but he got a smile back from her.

James relaxed.

Lace was back to flirting with Dave.

It was a wonderful meal. The food was delicious, and the company enjoyable. By dessert, the conversation had turned to Rae's book.

Rae didn't like being the center of attention; she was the one who preferred to listen. James found her slight blush tugging his protective nature.

He was pleased to hear that she had been

able to get an average six hours of writing time in each week since the vacation, and was now working on chapter twenty-four. When she talked about the book, she came alive in a way that made her face light up. He loved to see that expression.

They eventually moved to the living room and the baseball game, Lace accepting a small gesture from Dave to join him on the couch. Rae settled into a chair, and James sat across from her, watching her as much as he did the game.

Often, he would see her eyes drift from the game to the pictures on the mantel. She looked less hurt, but still sad.

It was not the time to ask her. He could have arranged a chance to ask her, but he didn't try. Tonight was not the right time.

There was a day coming soon that would be the right time. She needed to know a future did exist beyond what she presently had; she needed to know the sadness could be left behind and she could look at options beyond just her career. He had heard the weariness in her voice as she talked about how work was going, her progress in looking for a business partner.

She wasn't going to leave the sadness behind without someone taking the step to ask her on a date. He cared too much about her to leave for Africa without having helped her open that door.

He would be opening the door that someone else would eventually walk through.

He wanted her to still be single in five years, when he figured he would be coming back to the States for good. It wasn't fair to her. She wanted children. He had only to look at her at church around the children to see the obvious. It wasn't fair to rob her of a dream just because he would prefer to have her wait for him.

The sixth day working on the house was a physically challenging day. It was a hot, eighty degrees by 10:00 a.m., the sun and heat and humidity making them sweat and go through gallons of ice water. James paused on the bandsaw, having cut the last lumber they would need to finish framing in the master bedroom and master bath. Wearily, he wiped the sweat from his face with the towel he had slipped in his back pocket.

The pain was back.

He had woke to it that morning, a burning sensation in his chest muscles that had made him groan as he moved to get out of bed. It was mild compared to what it had been like in the past, but after two weeks without feeling it, it had been a surprise.

A hot shower had eased the pain, so that by the time he reached the site that morning he could almost believe he had imagined it. Almost.

He was going back. He was determined to be back in Africa on schedule. The pain this morning had only strengthened his resolve.

He didn't have to be a hundred percent to do the job. A little stiffness of a morning was something that could be managed.

It was coming up on four o'clock. He had worked through the day, able to do his job, and do it well. His work hadn't suffered, and the activity had not made the ache worse. This morning was a slight glitch, but not something that was going to stop him. Still, he was grateful when Kevin suggested they call it a day. He would spend the evening resting, and tomorrow would be better.

"James, Rae is going to be coming over for dinner tonight. She and I need to talk about the upcoming children's musical. Are you going to be in tonight? Should I set you a place?"

James paused as he reached for a soda can on the bottom shelf of the refrigerator. Trust his mom to act before he did. He retrieved a drink and popped open the tab. "I'll be in," he replied, smiling; he reached around her to swipe a finger across the edge of the icing bowl.

"You're as bad as the children," she scolded, smiling.

"I like fudge icing." She had baked a chocolate cake that afternoon.

"You've got your father's sweet tooth. Go see what kind of mail we got today," she asked, banishing him from her domain.

James kissed her cheek. "Sure, match-maker."

He met Rae at the door two hours later. She was tired, he saw that immediately, and while she had changed into jeans and a short-sleeve top, it was clear she had come immediately from work. "Come on in, Rae, Mom's in the kitchen. What can I get you to drink?"

She gave a grateful smile. "Iced tea, please."

She followed him to the kitchen, greeted his mom and pulled out a chair at the table, sat down. James watched her try to push the fatigue back, focus on his mom and the conversation.

He got her the drink she had requested, then pulled out the chair across from her, and settled back to watch and listen.

It didn't take long for her and his mom to come up with a plan for the children's musical, agree on who each one of them would call and recruit to help.

When dinner was served, Rae did her best to convey her appreciation to his mom, but James noticed that she barely ate. The phone rang soon after dessert was served. His mom waved him back to his seat and went to answer it.

"What happened today, Rae? You look . . . shell-shocked for want of a better word."

"I lost two hundred fifty thousand dollars," she replied. He heard the shock in her voice. "The last hour, the markets simply fell apart."

"Rae, I am sorry." He had no way to convey how deep his empathy went for the type of day she had obviously had.

She spun the ice in her water glass, her thoughts obviously a long way away. "We haven't had this bad a day in three years."

"Are you going to be okay?"

She gave a rough laugh. "I'm petrified of tomorrow. Hardly what my clients would want to hear me say tonight."

James pushed back his chair. "Come on, let's go for a walk."

It was a sign of how hard the day had been that she didn't even ask why. James interrupted his mom softly to tell her where they were going, and ask if she wouldn't mind fixing a piece of the cake for Rae to take home with her. He was worried about how little Rae was eating, but it didn't make sense to push it tonight.

The sun was getting ready to set. James watched Rae tuck her hands into the pockets of her jeans. Walking beside him, a weariness made her shoulders droop. "It's a beautiful sunset," he remarked quietly.

It got her to look up and notice. "Yes, it is."

James wanted to reach over and tuck her hand in his, tell her it would be okay. He couldn't. He had to settle for what he could do. The first thing to do was get her back in a positive frame of mind. "Okay, what's your game plan for tomorrow?"

She smiled, resigned. "I don't have one yet."

He slipped his hands into his own pockets and hid a wince at the way his left wrist complained in pain. "What are your options?"

"Sell and take profits before the stocks slide further. Do nothing. Sell strategically and use the cash to buy stocks that seem to be below their worth."

"How are you going to decide which one to do?"

She shrugged, then stopped walking for a moment, bit her bottom lip. "It hinges around one conclusion. I've got to decide if this is a short-term adjustment, or the warning shot of a long-term correction."

She started walking again, and he shortened his stride to hers. "Which do you think it is?"

"I don't know, James. I'm not current with my overall analysis, I don't have the facts I need to support a call either way. I'm kicking myself for being so careful to do the trading correctly, that I had not left adequate time to prepare for this. James, I cut my analysis time back so I could work on my book. Finding those six hours a week to write just burned my clients."

She was wrong. Those six hours of time writing had kept her able to do the trading and the analysis. They had kept her from burning out.

"What would Leo do in this situation?"

"He would be selling and taking profits, using the cash to go back into the market, buy stocks that slipped too far in the correction."

"Are you comfortable doing that?"

"Not at the speed he would do it. I don't know when a stock that is sliding down should be bought. I end up buying too early and having to watch it slide further before it bottoms out."

A slight breeze rustled through the branches and leaves of the trees they were walking under. It was an older neighborhood, the sidewalks lined with fifty-year-old oaks.

"You need to decide on a course for tomorrow, and go with it. When you have more information then you can adjust your plan," James said.

"Thanks." Rae nodded and lightly touched his arm.

They walked in silence for most of the way around the block and soon they were back to his mom's house.

"Would you like to go see some puppies?" James asked, wanting to distract her when he saw her frown at something she thought of.

His suggestion accomplished his goal; it broke her focus on her job. "I love puppies," she replied, slightly wistful.

"I know where there is a litter of four puppies, recently born. It's a five minute drive. Would you like to go?"

She nodded.

Pleased, James gestured to his car. "Come on."

The kennel was quiet.

James saw Rae look around with interest as they walked through the quiet hall toward the back of the building. "Never been here before?"

"No."

"I'll show you around later," James offered.

He opened the gate and was not able to stop a wince of pain at the action.

"James, what's wrong?" Rae had seen the pain cross his face.

When he didn't answer, her face grew more intent as she made her own conclusions. "Your wrist hurts, doesn't it? Your wrist hurt when you opened the gate." There was alarm in her voice.

"Rae, it's nothing. My body is stiff after a long day working on the house. That's all."

"That's not all it is. You winced, James."

"It's nothing, Rae," he insisted, stepping through the gate to the kennel runs and waiting for her join him.

"James . . ."

He smiled. "Rae, I promise, it's nothing. I'm fine. Come see the puppies."

Margo had the first kennel run, a spacious indoor and outdoor kennel she could move between at will. The dog was awake, having heard them enter the building. She was stretched out on a soft quilt, four furry bundles sprawled around and over each other asleep beside her.

"They're beautiful."

James opened the gate and felt the pain burn in his left wrist but refused to let any indication show on his face. "Hi, girl. How are you tonight?"

Margo raised her head and her tail began to beat against the blanket. James stroked her fur, greeted her as the old friend she was.

Rae knelt down beside him, cautiously offered her hand to Margo to inspect, had it licked in approval.

Two of the puppies stirred and tried to get up, only to roll as they tangled each other up. James laughed and caught them.

"This is Benjamin, and this is Justin."

Rae sat down on the kennel floor and Benjamin came over to climb in her lap. The puppy yawned and Rae laughed. "They are adorable, James."

James sat against the concrete wall and stretched his legs out, Justin in his lap. "I thought you might like them," he replied, rubbing Margo's coat and playing tug-of-war with the puppy over ownership of a towel.

The stress he had seen on Rae's face over dinner had eased. She was absorbed in the

146

puppy she held. James smiled. He was glad she had agreed to come. Now if he could only convince her to take a puppy home . . . Nothing made a stressful day fade faster than an animal that wanted all your attention. He laughed as the puppy tried to figure out how to get his front paw inside her jeans pocket.

"How are you doing this morning?" Kevin asked.

Kevin's question pulled James away from his thoughts. "Ready to get to work," he replied. He was going to need the time today working on the house to sort out his confusing thoughts from last night. He had loved the couple of hours he'd spent with Rae, walking with her, playing with the puppies, watching her. It had been a night he really enjoyed, and when she had left for home about nine, he had been able to tell the break had helped her, too. She'd left in a positive frame of mind, relaxed. For a while he had regretted Africa, until perspective cut back in, late that night.

He doubted a carpenter would be her first choice of a guy to date. With her background, her interests, a doctor or lawyer would be a better fit. He had never been one to hold a dream that did not have at least a corner of it rooted in reality. He had enjoyed the night and he hoped to enjoy another like it before he left for Africa, but that was the sum total of what he would hope for.

Kevin smiled. "Then let's do it."

James looked at the framed-in house. He was going to build this house and then he was going to go back to Africa. It mattered to him. He was going to make it happen. No matter what it took.

His wrist twinged as he grasped the ladder rung.

"Rae, how are you doing?"

Dave's call had been transferred to the war room, and his voice distracted her momentarily from the numbers she was studying.

"Dave, it's chaos. I'm busy and it's going to be a long day. Say a prayer for your finances, I'm currently losing your money." She winced as another group of numbers caved in and went red. "Anything you need?"

"For you to relax. You'll do fine. We'll bring dinner by the office around six."

Rae smiled. "Thanks, friend."

She leaned back in her chair to drop the phone in its cradle.

It was like trying to patch together a

leaking dam with bandages, the cracks in the market were spreading so rapidly. She was grateful she had made the assumption she was looking at the beginning of a major market correction, at least that decision was proving to be accurate.

"Scott, let's start moving about forty percent of the airline stocks to cash," she said quietly, mentally reviewing the holding lists for where her profits were the most vulnerable to the correction.

Some positions she was selling today had been held for five years, bought during the last major correction. Sooner or later, everything changed. Today had become that day.

She was playing it very conservative, choosing to ride it out and do nothing in most of the stocks she held, making moves only where it seemed strategically beneficial. It was going to be a long day.

"Rae's got a nice location," James commented, following Dave across the atrium of a major office complex. The building interior was marble, gold, modern, with plants and a multilevel waterfall.

"The builder of the complex was a friend of Leo's," Dave replied. "She's on the fifth floor."

A small sign by the suite door, stenciled in gold, told him they had arrived at Rae's office.

The reception area was a formal living room, with comfortable couches, chairs, and a glass-topped table set discretely to the side. "Lace decorated for them," Dave commented, smiling. He indicated the hall to the right. It opened into a large spacious room that was obviously the hub of the research area. The lady filing reports smiled when she saw them. "Hi, Dave."

"Hi, Janet. Have you met James, yet?"

"Not officially, no. Hello, James."

"It's nice to meet you, Janet."

"Where would you like the dinner we brought?" Dave asked, looking around.

She nodded to the conference room behind him. "Over there would be wonderful. We appreciate it. We're all behind today, there was so much happening so quickly."

"Where is she?"

"The war room."

"Any screams during the day?"

"She's been so calm you would think the market was flat," Janet replied.

"How did she do?"

Janet grinned. "Unbelievably well."

"She made money?"

"It's a tad insulting that you sound so surprised," Rae commented, causing Dave to look around.

"I brought pot stickers. Forgiven?"

She smiled and joined them. "Depends on how many you brought. Hi, James."

"Hi, Rae." She looked exhausted. It had obviously been a long stressful day, but her smile told him a lot about how she felt. She had done well today.

"Would you like a fast tour while I find everyone?"

"Sure."

"Dave, what should I bring you to drink?"

"Something cold."

Rae laughed. "I think I've got that. Janet?"

"A cream soda."

Rae pointed out doors as they walked back toward the reception area. "This is primarily the analysis wing of the suit, my office, another conference room, Janet's office." She took a turn just before she reached the reception area. "This is the trading wing, Leo's office. Scott — one of my key traders — Ann and Jeanna." She paused by one of the doors. "This is the trading room. I'll warn you in advance, it's normally a little neater."

She pushed open the door. James stepped inside. The amount of information and how it was correlated and displayed was incredible. It was like nothing he had ever seen before. He felt slightly overwhelmed. This was her domain?

"Rae, do you want to clear the rest of the position in five-year treasuries tomorrow? There is a working spread we could take advantage of," a man in his early twenties asked from the far side of the room.

"Punch it up to the monitors," she requested. He pressed a couple keys and the data he was looking at appeared on the main screen in front of her. Rae studied the data, nodded. "Good idea. Put them on the list to move early in the day. Scott, have you met James?"

"Spoken on the phone, but no. It's nice to meet you, James."

James shook hands, liking the man on sight. Dave spoke highly of him. "Same here. This looks like an interesting place to work."

Scott laughed. "Challenging," he replied.

"Dinner is here," Rae commented, picking up the stacks of notes she had scrawled during the day. "What can I get you to drink, Scott?"

He gestured to the table behind him. "Got it covered, Rae. The main conference room?"

Rae nodded.

"Give me another couple minutes to

finish the file transfers, and I'll be there."

"This has been a long day for you," James commented as they stepped into a small kitchen. It was six-thirty and Dave had mentioned Rae had called him from the office at 5:00 a.m. that morning.

Rae opened the refrigerator to get the requested drinks. "It will take a couple hours longer to wrap up today than usual, but seven o'clock isn't that uncommon. Did the building go okay today? I was worried about you."

James smiled as he took the drinks, careful in how he gripped the cans because his hands wanted to drop them. There was no way he was going to even hint how harsh the day had been. He had a weekend to relax and recuperate. The pain that had been in his ribs the day before had settled into all his joints with the viciousness of a disease that had never left.

But he had worked through the pain again, and it had not crippled him. It was different now; he knew what to expect, he knew how to adapt.

"We put the roof joists in place today. The work is going well. I've missed it Rae, building a place."

"I'm glad you're able to do it again. The pain is okay?"

"I'm fine," he replied.

She hesitated, then nodded. "Let's go eat."

It was a fair day — sunny, moderate temperature, slight breeze. A builder's ideal day. James was on the roof with Kevin laying the roof sheeting in place. They had set the joists that morning and by evening should be ready to lay the shingles. James slipped yet another nail from the bag and held it in place. He had been using the nail gun across the seams, but there were some corners that required a hand-driven nail.

Pain radiated through his entire body with every blow of the hammer.

The weekend had only let his joints grow more stiff, the pain more severe. It was a losing battle, and James knew it, but wouldn't let himself admit it.

He was losing a dream and he refused to simply give up.

Six months ago he would have thought nothing of laying the entire roof sheeting by hand. There was rarely electricity to power tools where his crews worked. James pulled another nail from the bag. The sweat was pooling around his eyes, sweat from the pain and not the physical labor.

He was not going to let this disease win. The nail dropped from fingers that could not hold it in place and he sighed heavily, hating the pain, hating the way his body was letting him down. He reached for another nail and tightened his grip on it, hating the burning pain that flared in his muscles in response to the action.

Kevin took the hammer out of his hand. "It is not going to help to let the pain cripple you."

James wanted to swear at his helplessness but it was intangible; Kevin was there. "Give me the hammer back, Kevin."

"It's not the end of the world if you can't be a builder anymore."

"I am a carpenter, Kevin. That is who I am." His anger was hot, directed at the illness, at his friend for putting into words what he knew but had not been willing to admit.

"There was a day Jesus walked away from his carpentry shop and did not go back. You've got to let it go, James. It looks like God has got other plans for you."

James had seen the grim look on his friend's face that morning. Kevin had been observing him for days. He knew the reality. James could deny the pain to his family, but Kevin knew better. It was minor consolation that his friend looked as pained by the reality as James felt.

James walked to the edge of the roof and took the ladder back down to the ground. Tired, exhausted, hurting and deeply discouraged, he pulled off his work gloves and unbuckled the tool belt he wore.

Kevin joined him. "James, this is not the end of the world. You just need more time."

"It's been six months, Kevin. Just how much longer do you suppose it will be before I can hold a hammer again for any length of time, be useful on a site?" James replied, feeling his body fighting against the pain in his joints. It was so crippling he would be lucky to be able to move tomorrow.

"It takes more than sweat equity to build a house."

"I'm not the type to be behind a desk, Kevin," James replied, angry at the situation, the brutal unfairness of it. He was good at what he did. The clinics he helped build saved lives. He loved the work. And the most black reality he had ever looked at was staring him in the face.

He wouldn't be going back.

Chapter Seven

✝

"James?" The soft voice called from the front of the kennels.

James rested his arms across his knees, and three puppies immediately attacked the towel that no longer moved. The fourth puppy was over by the gate, growling at a grasshopper that had dared to enter their playground. Margo was stretched out beside him, keeping watch on all her children.

"Back here, Rae." This was the very last thing he wanted. He did not want to see her, he did not want to see any of his friends.

It had been three days. He supposed he should be grateful they had waited this long. He glanced at his watch. It was after seven o'clock. His mood had been so black, the pain so great, his anger so hot, that for the past few days he had tried to make himself scarce. His friends didn't need to be around this.

He had left the doctor's office this afternoon and come to the kennel. Puppies didn't know how hard life could be; they only knew how to play and sleep and eat. They were good company — they didn't ask how he was doing, and he didn't have to tell them.

The disappointment was overwhelming, to know his dream was over. He wanted to go back. It wasn't easy to set aside that disappointment and act polite, friendly, calm. The last thing he wanted to hear was that this was God's plan. James couldn't believe this disease was part of God's plan. He might have permitted it, and He would eventually make some good come out of the situation, but it didn't make sense as part of His original plan.

He understood now Rae's comment that she wanted the past back. Leo had died young and Rae's dreams had been ripped away. This disease would hit and take away his dreams. The reality of such losses was heartbreaking.

"Hi," Rae said softly, stepping outside to join him in the fenced-in run.

He was tired — tired of the situation, tired of the pain, tired of wondering what he was going to do now. But when he saw her, he smiled. He was glad to see her. He had missed her.

She had changed into jeans and an over-size Chicago Bulls T-shirt. She sat down on the grass near him, and the puppies tumbled over to join her.

She didn't say anything, just sat playing with the puppies. He sat and watched her and was grateful.

He carefully rubbed his aching wrist. Even playing tug-of-war with a puppy was too much strain. He wondered who had called her. He had told his mom and Patricia about his doctor's appointment before calling and having a long talk with Bob. Dave had probably heard from Kevin, and from there Lace and Rae would have heard.

James had no idea what had happened with the markets these past two days, didn't know what Rae had been trying to deal with. He knew she had spent the weekend at work. He should have at least caught the evening news the last few days. He wasn't being much of a friend.

She looked weary. The kind of weariness that came from carrying a heavy load for a long time without a break.

One of the puppies tried to eat her shoe-laces. James reached over and pulled the puppy over to him, offering the towel as compromise.

"Thanks."

James smiled. "Sure."

She looked at him, wanting to say something. James took pity on her, opened the door she needed. "I called Bob, canceled my plane tickets."

"I heard," she said quietly. "I'm sorry, James."

He knew she was. Of all his friends, she was the one most able to understand and empathize with the loss. "How have the markets been this week?"

"Ugly."

She didn't say anything else, and James knew her struggle to keep her job to sane limits was being lost. "How many hours has it been this week, Rae?"

"At the office from 5:00 a.m. to about 7:00 p.m., followed by late evenings at home trying to get the analysis work done. I am so tired of work."

No time to work on her book, that went without saying. "I'm sorry, Rae."

She smiled. "We've both got pretty big burdens to carry this month. I know you need some space for a few days, but I desperately needed a break, that's why I decided to come by."

"Rae, I'm glad you did. I'm not exactly good company right now, but I am glad to see you."

She helped a puppy settle in her lap. "Dave is dragging me to a baseball game Sunday afternoon. Would you like to come?"

He considered it for a few moments. "Yes."

She smiled. "Good."

"Have you had dinner yet, Rae?"

She blinked, surprised to realize she had not. "I meant to, but no. I think I left a plate of pasta in the microwave."

James chuckled. "Come on, I'll buy you a hamburger at the diner down the block. I want some ice cream and they make an awesome sundae."

He expected her to decline, pleading lack of time or that she was not hungry or something. Her silence did last a few beats too long, but she nodded yes.

"Should we put the puppies inside?"

"Margo will corral them inside when she's ready for them to settle down," James replied. His body argued in pain as he moved to stand up, making him clench his jaw. Rae saw, but didn't say anything. She did maneuver to be the one who opened the gate. James was almost grateful — almost. He intensely disliked needing the help.

The diner was a locally owned, popular place. It was late enough in the evening they were seated almost immediately. Rae glanced at the menu and ordered a bowl of soup and a salad. James frowned, but didn't say anything. She was losing weight; she needed to eat more.

"I don't want to talk about work, and you don't want to talk about the pain. So what do we talk about?"

"Dave and Lace?" James offered with a smile.

Rae grinned. "A favorite subject. I hear they actually went out on a date last night."

"Really?"

"Lace called me shortly before midnight. She woke me up — had to tell me all about it."

"Let me guess, a museum showing?"

"Actually, dinner with a private collector Dave had met a year ago at a conference."

"I'm glad. They make a good couple."

"Do you really think Dave is ready to settle down? Lace has had a crush on him for so long, she doesn't need to get hurt by being one of a list."

James thought about it. "He's ready to settle down. It's in all the little things he does, the way he looks at her, the way he talks about kids."

"Dave being a dad. That I never expected to see."

"What about Lace? Does she want kids?"

"Very much. I think that's why she started dating the tax attorney — she knows her time is running out."

James wanted to know what Rae thought about the subject of children. She was the same age as Lace, so it had to be a concern for her as well. Had she written off that dream when Leo died? It would be a shame if she had. Rae would make a good mom.

Her meal and his ice cream arrived and neither one said much as they ate.

Did this constitute a date? James wondered as Rae pushed aside her soup and salad, both only half-eaten.

"Not hungry?"

"Food doesn't settle well anymore," she admitted. She gave a rueful smile. "Lace will kill me if I've developed an ulcer."

"Rae . . ."

"Don't push, James. I'll deal with it."

"Do it soon," he insisted.

"Yeah. I hate doctors."

He smiled. "Now that I can understand."

She realized what she had said, smiled back. "I bet you do."

She glanced at her watch and sighed. "I've got to go. Work is waiting."

James knew ignoring the work was simply an option Rae didn't have. "Rae, remember

163

to pace yourself, okay?"

"I'm trying. Honestly."

He walked back with her to the kennel and to her car. He said goodbye with surprising reluctance.

It was a quiet spot, a bench in a local park that could look down on a ball field or over to a small playground, a place to pause and rest during a walk. James sat down, physically needing the break. He was trying — trying too hard — to exercise enough to keep his body improving, but not too much to cause more damage.

The recuperation was slow at best.

He sat down and carefully stretched his legs out.

God, I don't understand.

I loved Africa. I loved serving people, building clinics, saving children's lives. Now Father, here, I don't have a purpose. I don't even know where to begin.

I don't understand why You ended such a long ministry in such an abrupt way. Why not some warning? Why not a sense that maybe I should start thinking about coming back to the States? Why so abrupt? One day I'm fine, the next week I'm in so much pain I can barely move. I feel like You abandoned who I was and what I was doing. You didn't give me closure,

Lord, You just took the ministry away.

What am I suppose to do in the States?

If You've taken away my ability to hold a hammer and saw, You've pretty much taken away who I am.

You have thousands of good architects here, Lord, thousands of good builders. Why take away a ministry that was doing some good for people?

I don't understand.

All my life, even through the rough times, I have known You had a plan. For the first time, here, now, it feels like You've forgotten me.

The sun woke him Saturday morning, the light streaming into the bedroom and making him blink as he tried to read the time.

He moved cautiously to pull over a pillow, take the strain off his neck. His joints were stiff, his spine taut, but the burning pain was not as severe. James had begun to dread the first hour after he woke up, he was grateful that today was not as bad as the other mornings had been this last week. Time and rest were beginning to ease the symptoms.

If he was staying in the States, what did he want?

It had taken days to shake off the anger,

the frustration of the situation and face the reality.

If he was staying in the States, what did he want to do?

It was time to accept reality and go on.

If he was building a new life in the States, then it was time to do it and quit wishing for what was not going to happen. Returning to Africa was not in his future.

He lay in bed looking at the ceiling, thinking.

Buy a house with a yard, that was definite.

Kevin wanted him to take over some of the architecture work and the idea was worth considering. He could work from home, do it at a pace he could tolerate.

Rae. He wanted to get to know her. More than just the surface he knew now. He liked her. He liked the twinkle in her eyes, her smile, her laugh, her willingness to do what was required despite the personal costs.

He didn't want to be alone anymore.

It was a big aching hole in his gut. He didn't want to be alone anymore. If he was back, then he wanted what he had been delaying and saying "not yet" to for years — marriage and a family.

Patricia was due in mid-January. James knew seeing the baby was going to bring back lots of memories. It had been his favorite part of Africa, seeing the children at the clinics.

Rae liked kids. At church most Sundays he found her in the nursery, and the wistfulness in her eyes had not escaped him. She would like to be a mom.

Leo was a big problem. The sadness hadn't left Rae's eyes yet. She was still locked in the past, still grieving. The grief was easing, but it was still there. James wasn't sure how to help her, how to ease that pain she carried.

He had to wait for his own health to stabilize again, but give him a few weeks and he would be fit again. He had to be. He could not imagine life where this pain didn't eventually ease off. Three weeks to get Rae to say yes to a date. He had faced tougher assignments, not many, but a few.

She was an avid White Sox fan.

James looked over at her, surprised, when she stood up and yelled to get the attention of the third base player. The man turned, found them, smiled, waved back.

Dave looked around her. "Before he moved downtown, he used to hang out with us," he explained.

James nodded, somehow not surprised.

Rae sat down again, and James reached

over to snag the drink she was waving around. "You're surprising me," he commented with a smile.

"Really? That's good," she replied, a twinkle in her eyes.

She leaned back and put her feet on the empty seat in front of her, picked up her binoculars again. They were five rows behind the White Sox bench; the binoculars were not really necessary.

It was a good day, with good company. Lace was somewhere, having disappeared to find nachos. Lace had hugged him when she saw him. The hug had hurt, but James had no intention of ever mentioning that, pleased to have her acknowledge without words what had happened. He had grinned when Lace had maneuvered them so Rae was sitting next to him.

James relaxed in the seat, stretching his legs out as best he could. The pain was moderate today, manageable.

They went out to eat after the game, an early dinner. Lace took them to a new Mexican place she had found. Rae, sitting in the seat beside him at the table, competed with him for the dish of hot sauce for the tortilla chips. "Rae, this is going to make your stomach a mess," James cautioned quietly.

She hesitated over a chip. "You're right.

But I could be wrong about the problem. I'll risk it."

By the end of the meal, James could tell she was regretting the risk. Her face was pale and she had pulled back from the conversation.

"Dave, Lace, I hate to be the one to break up a party, but Rae and I have plans. We need to be going."

Rae looked at him, surprised, but didn't hesitate to take the silent offer, getting up and pushing back her chair.

"Stay and enjoy dessert," he told Lace and Dave, smiling at the surprised look on both their faces.

"Of course," Dave replied, smiling. "I'll pick up the tab for dinner, go enjoy the night."

"Thanks," James replied, wishing it really was what he was trying to imply.

"Date?" James saw Lace ask Rae silently.

Rae just smiled and picked up her handbag. James quietly moved back to let her precede him as they walked through the restaurant tables. She hesitated as they stepped outside, looked around the parking lot. James reached for her hand and was shocked to find how cold and clammy it was. He looked at her, alarmed.

He put his arm around her waist and

walked her across the parking lot to his car.

"That was so stupid . . ."

He carefully tucked her into the passenger seat, clipped on her seat belt. He could hear the self-directed anger. "Relax, Rae. It was a mistake, not a crisis."

As he drove, she leaned her head back against the headrest, closed her eyes, fought to keep her stomach from cramping. James settled his hand across her clenched ones. "Don't forget to breathe, Rae."

She gave a tight laugh. "It hurts."

James's hand tightened. "I know."

He thought about stopping somewhere, a pharmacy, a drugstore, to find something that might help, but he didn't know where one would be in this area and the car ride was not helping her. Getting her home seemed more important. There were stores near her town house; he would get her settled in her own home, then swing back to the store to pick up something that might help her.

She had been quiet for too long, and her hands were damp with sweat. "Doing okay?"

"I feel awful," she replied softly, not opening her eyes.

James squeezed her hands, hurting for her.

He pulled into the drive at her town house behind her Lexus, came around to open the door for her. He watched her take a deep breath before she moved, and saw her wince as she stood.

"Where are your keys?"

She found them in her bag.

He unlocked the door, stepped inside and made a sweeping inspection to make sure the place looked undisturbed. "Do you have something or should I go down to the pharmacy?"

"Buy me some of that pink stuff if nothing else," she asked, grateful. She eased off her shoes. "I'm going to go lie down."

He carefully brushed her damp forehead with his hand. "I'll be back as quick as I can, Rae."

"Go on, I'm okay."

He gave a soft smile. "Sure you are."

He locked the door behind him, taking Rae's keys with him. Ten minutes later he was back at Rae's, unlocking the front door.

"Hey, Lady," he called softly. She was not downstairs stretched out on the couch, so he walked quietly up the stairs.

The master bedroom was at the end of the landing, a large room, decorated in several shades of deep green and gold. A beautiful and neat room. Rae was lying on the comforter, curled up slightly, her knees pulled up.

"I brought you some stuff," James said, sitting down carefully beside her.

She opened her eyes cautiously. "Thank you." The words were barely a whisper.

James gently stroked her hair back. She looked so different from the lady in control he had come to know. He opened the sack and read directions, found the bottle that promised to act the quickest. "Let me get you something to drink to take this with."

"There's a glass in the bathroom."

James ran the tap until the water was cold, filled the glass.

"See if this helps."

She gratefully took the medication he offered, then lay back down. She was shivering. James reached over and caught hold of the end of the comforter, then folded it up around her to keep her warm.

"James, at the restaurant . . . how did you know?"

"You were turning the color of unsalted butter," he replied, smiling, glad to have her somewhere she could rest and recover.

"Thanks for what you did."

"Don't mention it," he replied gently. "Need some soda, something else to help?"

She shook her head. "I don't think I'll risk it."

She grew quiet and James sat beside her on the bed, idly smoothing her hair with his hand, watching her, thinking.

"I can't miss work tomorrow."

James hesitated. "You just took the medicine, Rae. In a couple of hours you will feel much better."

"Have to be," she replied, her voice slurring slightly as she grew drowsy.

"If something really bad happened and you couldn't go in to work, what would you do?"

"Dave has power of attorney, and Jack would step in, manage the accounts temporarily until I was back or Dave could arrange a more permanent situation."

She stirred restlessly. "Hot."

James pushed the comforter back. Within moments she was cold again.

"My stomach wants to be sick," she warned him, groaning suddenly as she coiled up again.

He rubbed her back.

"You'll survive," he replied, glad he had stayed, glad she had not made a big deal of his staying.

She was on her feet a few minutes later, staggering to the bathroom, waving him away. He ignored her wishes, staying with her to keep her hair back as she was violently sick. He handed her mouthwash and used a hand towel to gently wash her face.

He tucked a blanket around her shivering frame and sat with her on the bathroom floor, leaning against the wall. "You're off Mexican food for a while," he told her firmly, rubbing her icy hands briskly between his.

She was buried in the blanket, her head tucked against his chest. "Not a problem," she agreed with a weak laugh.

James hated seeing anyone sick, but it certainly was one way to get her to forget her normal reserve around him. When he let go of her hands, she curled them against his chest, gave a soft sigh.

James rested his arms around her waist and waited for her to feel better, to risk moving back to the bed to lie down. He liked having her in his arms.

"Going to sleep?" he asked, amused, when she was still leaning against him motionlessly several minutes later. She was almost limp.

He felt her relax at the amusement in his voice. "Hardly. Not on the bathroom floor. Although I have been known to drift off if I'm somewhere warm and comfortable. I don't care how good the movie is, chances are I'm going to fall asleep."

James tightened his arms and really considered kissing the top of her head. "I'll remember that."

"I like mushy movies." He could hear the amusement in her voice, and a yawn that cracked her jaw.

"Does this mean if I ask you on a date, you might say yes?"

"Depends on what, where and when," she finally replied.

"Tomorrow night, Shaw's, eight o'clock?"

"Day after. Eight o'clock is fine."

He smiled. "You've got a date."

She nodded. "Good."

They sat together in silence, Rae trying to drift off to sleep and James content to hold her and think. A few more minutes and he would urge her back to bed where she could rest in better comfort. For now, here was just fine.

She suddenly stiffened. "Let me up."

She jerked forward.

She was sick again.

He felt her spine ripple with the spasms. "Easy, Rae, easy. Don't fight it."

He was helpless other than supporting her weight. He hated this. There were tears running down her face now. He gently wiped them away, eased her back onto the floor when the worst was past.

Whatever medicine she had taken earlier had been lost, but he couldn't risk giving her more. She protested weakly when he eased her out of his arms, forgave him when a cold cloth pressed against her cheeks.

"Don't tell Dave about this. I'll never hear the end of it."

"I won't," he promised softly.

He eased her into bed twenty minutes later when it looked as if she were past the worst. She sank back into the covers, her eyes closed. A nightgown and the lights off would be a lot more conducive to rest, but he didn't intend to leave until she had more medicine and was clearly feeling better.

His own body was aching with the unforgiving costs of sitting on the floor. He pulled over the chair she had in the room, silently scanned the stack of books she had beside her bed. Most were medical texts, but he found a Spencer mystery and pulled it from the stack. It was a good book, but he read only a few pages at a time, as he quietly watched Rae, worried about her.

The picture beside her bed . . . *the ring* . . . held his attention for a long time. It was a beautiful ring, hanging from a ribbon looped over the picture frame.

What had it been like to be handed that ring after Leo had died, to have such a tangible indication of how much had been ripped away? Was it a comfort to have his picture, the ring in sight each night, or was it making it harder to let go and move on? He looked at the ring and back at Rae and felt slightly sick himself. She might say yes to a date, but she was a long way from stepping beyond the past.

God, what's the key to get past her pain? You know. Will You help me understand how to help her let go of the past? At least not make it worse?

Finally toward midnight, he got more medicine in her. She seemed to be feeling better.

He eased the covers around her, leaned down and gently kissed her forehead. "Call me in the morning, Rae."

Her eyes were serious when they locked with his. "Thank you, James."

He looked back, just as serious. "Good night, Rae," he finally said. He reached over and clicked off the light. "Sleep well."

He pulled her door partly shut, took the book with him downstairs. He didn't want to leave until the medication had a chance to work.

She had said yes. He wanted to smile, to feel the anticipation, but the impulse was tempered by the fact that he knew how careful he needed to be. He couldn't afford a mistake with Rae. She had a lot to deal with without him making a careless comment and making things worse. She was a beautiful lady, a wonderful friend, someone he wanted to get to know at a much deeper level. He couldn't afford a mistake.

He left for home about one-thirty, Rae sleeping peacefully, her face looking relaxed in the moonlight.

Did she really want to date James?

Rae eased back against the counter, sipping her coffee, considering the question. She was in her robe and slippers; the dawn was still just a twilight. It was a quarter past five. She had allowed herself to sleep in an extra half hour, hoping her stomach would remain settled. So far, she felt a little tentative, but she was still on her feet.

She didn't want to date him.

It was her gut reaction — a strong one — not wanting to risk being vulnerable, not wanting to risk letting someone really get to know her. She had been down this road before, let Leo get close. Love was a powerful thing that made life so full of joy.

When you lost it . . . Rae didn't want to get hurt like that ever again.

Did she want to date James?

She didn't want to wake up alone for the rest of her life. She wanted someday to have a son, a daughter, someone to call her Mom. She wanted that.

To date James meant she had to risk getting hurt again.

Very rarely did she let herself think back to what the first year without Leo had been like. It was too painful, too raw, too black. She never wanted to experience that again. She didn't want to get near a situation like that ever again.

She rubbed her foot on the flooring, tracing a pattern in the tiles.

She didn't have a choice.

Of every man in her life, James was the only one she could see as potentially being her husband. She already had a crush on him, not that she would admit that to Lace. She liked him. She liked what he had done with his life, how he related to his family, who he was as a friend. She had been around him and she had been watching him. His faith and his actions were consistent with one another. His words and his actions were consistent. He would make a wonderful husband.

She was going to have to risk her heart — and hope and pray for the best.

"His car was still here at 1:00 a.m. It must have been quite a date."

Rae tried to reach the book she had just knocked behind the headboard. "Lace, it wasn't like you think." Her friend had shown up shortly after eight-thirty with a gallon of ice cream and a video they had not seen before, interrupting Rae in the middle of cleaning house.

Lace pulled yet another dress from the back of Rae's closet, considered it, and put it back with a slight shake of her head. "Oh, really? When are you seeing him again?"

Rae couldn't stop the blush.

"I thought so," Lace said, smiling. "When?"

"Tomorrow night," Rae finally admitted. "He's picking me up at eight."

"Casual or dressy?"

"Casual."

Lace went back to inspecting the contents of Rae's closet. "This might do," she finally decided, pulling out a green silk dress.

"That is not casual," Rae said.

"Casual means low heels, less jewelry. It is a simple dress that will go anywhere."

Rae bit her lip, considering. "Maybe, but

only if I can wear my hair down."

"It looks beautiful down. Wear that gold necklace Dave gave you for your birthday, and maybe the bracelet from Leo."

Rae considered, then moved past Lace to look for shoes. "These?"

"Perfect. Where are you going?"

"Shaw's."

"Nice place."

Rae wished she had said no when he asked her. An actual date. Maybe she could plead still feeling ill.

No. She was not a coward, even if she felt like one. She had another day to get over her nerves.

"What did you and Dave do last night after we left?"

Rae was astounded to see Lace blush. "Lace?"

"We went to see a movie."

"That hardly explains that blush," Rae said, sitting down on the side of the bed. "Give."

Lace sighed and sank down on the bed beside her, picked up the bear Leo had given Rae. "He kissed me."

"Dave."

Lace nodded. Her expression was so morose, Rae didn't know what to think.

"And?"

"And we're going to mess up a great friendship. He doesn't have a settle-down bone in his entire body."

"That's all?"

Lace nodded.

"Thank goodness. I was afraid for a moment. I thought it was a bad kiss."

"It was a great kiss," Lace said, more depressed.

"Dave really does want to settle down, Lace. He's just been kind of slow to realize that. He's been thinking about it lately, even thinking about having kids, if James is to be believed."

Lace visibly perked up. "Our Dave?"

Rae smiled. "One and the same."

"He could have mentioned that to me, the turkey."

Rae laughed. "We're suppose to be having a girls night, and here we are talking about guys. Come on, let's go watch that movie. I hear you need a box of tissues by the time it's over." She tugged Lace to her feet.

"Can I ask one more guy question?"

Rae hesitated. "Sure."

"James is a serious kind of guy, Rae. He isn't the type to date casually. Are you sure you know what you're doing? I don't want you to get hurt," Lace said softly.

"Lace, I'm scared to death that this is a mistake, but I said yes. I guess I'm going to find out."

"This house has the space you were looking for, James. And the yard. It needs work, but the structure is sound and the price is certainly right. I think you ought to buy it," Kevin concluded, standing on the drive and looking over the property again.

They had already been down in the crawl space, up in the attic, on the roof, done a detailed inspection. It was a good property.

"I'll think about it overnight, but I agree. This is the place." James looked over the house. His transition to the States was going to feel so finished the moment he bought a house. He would be settled here for the long-term. "You said the schools in the area are good?"

Kevin raised a single eyebrow at the question, but replied, "Excellent."

James nodded. He would be raising a family here, knowing about the schools was an important factor. The house had the room he would need to set up an office, let him resume work as an architect in a consulting capacity with Kevin. It had room for his wife to have a large office, and still leave bedrooms for children. There were some structural changes to be made — two walls would go when he remodeled — but it was a house with possibilities.

The yard needed work, but there was almost an acre of land. Plenty of room for kids to play.

What do You think, God? Is this the place to settle down and make a new start? It's certainly a wonderful place with great potential.

"You thinking about settling down in more ways than just buying a house?" Kevin asked.

James weighed how to answer. "Possibly," he hedged. He needed to get this bug back under control, work the pain out of his system again. He had done it once, he could do it again. He had been thinking a lot about a lady with twinkling blue eyes.

Kevin smiled. "Wonderful idea. I would act on it."

"I'm thinking about it," James replied, smiling.

She should have chosen a different dress. Rae turned one way and the next, trying to decide if this was really an acceptable choice. It was a beautiful dress. But she had bought it to wear to a concert with Leo. They had never gone, but still, it was a dress that had some history.

God, what do You think?

She had never been so nervous about a night in her life. At work it had been difficult, if not impossible to concentrate. The whole office had seemed to know that something was up.

God, I hope Your sense of humor holds. I'm probably going to need You to pull my foot out of my mouth a few times tonight.

She was blowing this out of proportion. It was a date, yes, but that was all it was. She needed to relax, quickly.

The doorbell rang, the chimes sounding throughout the house, and her muscles tensed. She forced them to relax.

She descended the steps, moved to the front door.

He stood in the doorway, relaxed and comfortable in dress slacks and a tailored shirt. "Hi."

It was the soft greeting, the relaxed way he smiled, that made her relax and smile back. "Hi, James."

"You look very nice tonight."

She blushed slightly, looked at the dress. "Thank you."

"Dave said roses and Lace said orchids, but I decided on something more unique." He picked up a bouquet of wildflowers from the rail. The flowers were delicate, fragile,

185

the bouquet a riot of color.

She accepted them, touched by the thought and the attention he had paid to the detail. Every color of a rainbow was present. "They are lovely, James."

"They are flowers whose beauty will eventually fade, your beauty won't."

Flowers she had expected . . . the compliment she had not. "James . . ."

He grinned. "It took two days to come up with the line, but I haven't had much practice in the last six years. My delivery still needs a little practice."

She leaned against the doorjamb, grinned. "Oh, I don't know. You did pretty well."

He reached out and touched her hand. "Go find a vase for the flowers and let's get this night underway."

She joined him a few moments later, carrying a lace wrap should the night turn cool.

He locked the front door for her.

Rae walked with him down the drive, liking the attention as his hand touched the small of her back, the fact he matched his pace to hers. "Can I ask one question, if I then promise to drop the subject for the night?"

He opened the car door for her, smiled. "Somehow I think I would prefer to have you ask it now, than have this question in your mind for the evening," he replied. He walked around the car, slipped behind the wheel, turned the key in the ignition. When the car was running, he rested his hands across the steering wheel and turned toward her. "What's your question, Rae?"

"How bad is the pain today?"

He nodded, conceding it was a good question. "On a scale of one to ten, one being so bad I don't want to move, ten being I no longer notice any symptoms, today is about a six."

He pulled out of the drive and headed toward the restaurant. "Can I ask one question, if I promise to stay off the subject for the rest of the evening?"

Rae hesitated before nodding. "I suppose fair says you get at least one."

He chuckled. "Tell me about work."

"That's a complex question. Anything specific you would like to know?" she asked, looking at him. She saw him nod.

"Do you still like your job?"

Rae leaned her head back against the headrest. "I love the challenge. I love the fact I am good at turning data into a concrete conclusion. There are times I even think I may learn to like the trading. But I hate the hours. There has been no time for the book lately, and I really hate that."

"Tonight is taking time away that you could be using to write."

Rae was grateful that he understood the cost she had paid when she said yes. "Yes. But I don't regret my choice."

"I'll make the night worth it."

Rae smiled. "It already is."

They arrived at the restaurant.

Rae took her time looking over the menu. "Do you think baked trout would be safe?"

He grinned. "I would say that is a good choice."

Rae liked the evening with him, sharing a meal. He told her stories about Africa, stories from the days working with Kevin building their business. He made her laugh and it made the stress of the workday fade.

They lingered at the restaurant for almost two hours, enjoying the chance to talk together. When James finally suggested they should consider leaving, she agreed, knowing she needed to call it a night before it got much later, but regretting the ending of a wonderful evening.

"Would you like to see someplace special?" James asked her as she fastened her seat belt.

She looked over at him, surprised. "Sure."

He nodded. "It's not far."

He took them to an established neighborhood a couple miles from her own home, where the trees were ancient and the houses set back on large plots of land. He drew to a stop in front of a two-story house, put the car in park.

Rae looked around with interest.

"My new place," James said quietly.

She turned to look at him. "Really?" He had bought a house? She looked back at the place. He had bought a place. A deep spot of uncertainty inside her dissolved. She had been afraid he might end up settling in a different city, with a different job. He had bought a house. This was good.

He smiled at her surprise. "Come on, I'll show it to you," he offered, turning off the engine.

Rae slipped out of the car.

It was a beautiful home. James had arranged to have the key and he opened the front door for her, gave her a guided tour, pointing out the structural changes he planned to make. Rae wandered around behind him, enjoying listening to James in his element, the house having replaced his discouragement with something positive.

They walked back to the car, James quiet and Rae enjoying the beautiful night.

It was eleven o'clock when James escorted her up the walk to her own front door. "I'm sorry I made it such a late night for you."

Rae leaned against the doorpost, not entirely ready to say good-night yet. "I'm not. I had a good time, James."

He rocked back on his heels, smiling. "So did I. Would you like to do it again?"

Rae considered the offer. "Would you like to come over for a movie Thursday night?"

He smiled at her. "You go to sleep with a movie."

"Only with guys I like."

He grinned. "What do you say I pick out the movie?"

"I like this plan."

"Say eight o'clock again? I'll bring dinner?"

"Deal." She smiled and reached forward, touched his hand. "Thank you, James."

His hand turned over and gently grasped hers. "Have a good night, Rae."

Chapter Eight

The ground was soft; it had rained during the night. Rae's heels sank into the grass as she crossed the landscaped grounds.

"Hi, Leo." She carefully settled on the bench near his headstone. "I've missed you."

It was a weekday morning, at an hour she should have been at the office. Instead she was at a cemetery, her beeper on, her cellular phone in her purse, trying to shake off the effects of a rough night of no sleep.

"I'm scared, Leo, and I don't know why."

The dreams had been nice, at first. She had been with James, she had been happy, she had been in the house she had visited, but the dreams had always ended with her being abandoned.

She sighed, and looked over the grounds, looked up at the beautiful sky. There were no answers to find here. She had thought the dreams reflected what she was still feeling from Leo's death, but she had been wrong. It was peaceful here today; there was sadness, but the grief was gone.

The grief had moved on without her realizing it.

The trip here had been worth that much at least. It was an hour's drive. She rarely came, instinctively knowing it was better to let the memories fade.

The troubled sleep did not originate from here.

The car ride back to the office was made with her thoughts deep in options. To think ahead for months at a time, to consider options, was part of both her personality and her training. She had some serious issues to resolve.

She was dating James. It had been one date so far, but he was buying a house nearby. Lace had read him right, he was not a man to date casually. The next several months were going to see a relationship being developed. Did she want that?

Yes. She had made that decision the night she had agreed to the first date.

A relationship meant time.

She still had a book to write. That book mattered to her, more than any of her friends understood.

No matter which way she laid out her

schedule, she simply did not have enough time to do her job, write a book, and get to know James. Something simply had to give.

The job.

She had to find a partner. She had to. It was that, or sell the business.

James was early.

Rae descended the steps quickly, paused at the bottom of the stairs, took a few deep breaths, trying to make her anticipation less obvious. She flipped the locks on the door.

"Hi." She was past the point of being nervous. She had missed him.

"Hi, lady."

His smile made her feel so good inside.

She held the door for him as he had his hands full. Something smelled wonderful.

"Mom was making Italian, so I brought us homemade ravioli."

Rae settled her hand on his arm and liked the strength she felt. She looked into the sack. "Cheesecake?"

"Homemade, too."

"You can bring dinner over whenever you would like."

He laughed. "Come on, let's eat while it's still hot."

Rae had struggled with how to set the table. She had wanted it to look nice, but not overly romantic. It was dinner and a movie. She had compromised with elegant place mats and her bouquet of flowers as the centerpiece.

James unpacked the sack. Salad, strawberries, ravioli, homemade rolls, cheesecake.

James told her about progress on the house purchase as they ate, and Rae told him about her day, glossing over the stress. It was a comfortable conversation, but it was impersonal, leaving Rae feeling slightly discontent.

They moved to the living room after dinner, James taking the remaining strawberries with them.

Rae hesitated for a moment, then chose the couch, pushing the coffee table out with her foot so she could sink down in the cushions and use the table as a footrest. "What movie did you end up choosing?"

He slipped it into the VCR, and used the remote to click on the television, set the volume. "An old one. A mushy one."

She blinked, surprised. "You got a mushy movie?"

He chuckled at her expression, nudged her over to free a pillow, sat down beside her. "It's a date, Rae. Mushy is good planning on my part."

"If it had not been a date?"

He stretched his legs out and grinned. "A Western, definitely."

Rae leaned against his shoulder. "I like Westerns, too," she whispered.

"Do you?"

"Anything but horror," she confirmed.

His hand gently brushed through her hair. She loved being this close to him, able to see the expression in his eyes, feel his chest rise and fall under her hand. The movie came on, interrupting the moment. She didn't move away; instead, settled against him. His arm slipped around her. His hand captured hers.

It was a love story.

Partway through the movie, Rae shifted to rest her head against his chest, snuggle her hands against his shirt, relax further as she watched, captivated by the story.

James's hand gently stroked her hair.

It was a movie that required a box of tissues.

She was crying toward the end but had no desire to disturb the pleasure of the moment with James. She was supremely comfortable, tucked in his arms.

James grabbed the tissue box and gently wiped her wet cheeks.

When it was over, she dropped her head

down against his chest, hiding her face. "Next time, don't get a mushy movie. I look awful when I cry," she said, laughing, as she tried to wipe away the damage.

James settled her against him. He studied her face seriously, smiled gently. "I think you look okay to me."

"You're being kind."

His hands brushed her cheeks dry. "No, I'm not," he said simply.

Rae eased her hands to his shoulders. "James."

"Hmm?" He drew her closer.

"Isn't this going pretty fast for a second date?"

"I've wanted to kiss you for about twelve weeks now, it feels kind of slow to me," he replied with a slow smile.

She blushed softly. "Really?"

He grinned. "Quit fishing for a compliment."

If she leaned forward even a little, they would be kissing. She wanted to kiss him too much to let herself do it.

She dropped her gaze. She wasn't used to this emotion.

"We need to take a walk," James said abruptly.

It took Rae a few moments to remember how to breathe again. He got up and held out his hand and she had to shake her head a couple of times to clear it before she could focus on his hand and accept it.

She steadied herself with a hand braced against his forearm. "A walk is a real good idea. Where are my shoes?"

Having him tie her tennis shoe laces helped break some of the tension inside her, the cool air outside helped finish the task.

James put his arm around her shoulders as they began walking down the block. Rae took advantage of the opportunity to tuck herself as close to him as she could get.

"It would have been quite a kiss," she offered, teasing softly.

He laughed. "Oh yeah, it would have been quite a kiss."

She wanted this relationship to progress. The realization made her shiver. Her mind was thinking marriage and children. It was too much transition. Fifteen weeks ago she had been grieving over Leo, thinking her life was over, and now she was at this point with another man.

She eased slightly away from him. "It's been almost two years since I kissed a guy."

"Try six years since I really kissed a lady," James replied. He let her ease away, but kept hold of her hand. "I think we would be wise to avoid the situation for a while."

They walked together in silence. Rae felt herself begin to relax again. Nothing had changed, not really. They were dating. They were both going to have to decide how serious they wanted the relationship to be, where it was heading, how fast it was going to move. It was good to know the potential for a lot more than just friendship was there.

"Rae?"

"Hmm?"

"Can I ask you a tough question?"

She turned and looked up at him, saw how serious he was. "Sure."

"Were you and Leo planning to have kids?"

Rae felt the wistfulness well back inside. "Yes," she whispered, looking out at the night. "At least three. He liked the idea of a big family."

James squeezed her hand. "I didn't mean to touch a raw memory."

"That's okay. We were planning it all, the house, the kids, the dog."

He tucked his arm around her again, pulling her close. "Tell me to butt out if you don't want to talk about this."

She nodded. "What do you want to know?"

"Has the anger faded?"

"At Leo?"

"And God."

Rae considered it as they walked. "Mostly. It's just a profound sense of disappointment that lingers now, that the dreams and plans ended so abruptly. How are you doing with losing Africa?"

"Resigned. There's nothing short of a miracle cure that can bring it back."

The silence stretched between them. Rae wished they were further along in the relationship so that she didn't feel so . . . awkward. She wanted to know what he thought about getting married, having kids . . . not necessarily with her, but in general, she told herself as she bit her bottom lip.

"What?" He sounded amused.

She looked up at him, this man she had dreamed about, had decided to let past her reserves to say yes to a date, to say yes to possibly a lot more. He was smiling at her.

"What question is circling around in that mind of yours, wanting to be asked?"

She blushed.

His expression grew serious and gentle. He brushed her cheek with a finger. "It's okay. Ask."

"Did you buy that house planning to have children?"

"Four," he replied, smiling. "At least two adopted. I've got a wallet full of snapshots of children, I want a few of my own to add to the collection."

"Four."

James tugged her hair lightly. "My wife will have a little say, of course."

"That's kind of necessary," Rae reminded him, grinning. So what if it was only a second date? Nothing had been conventional in her life or in their relationship to this point. She might as well ask the questions she would like to have answers to. "What's your ideal honeymoon?"

Her question amused him. "That's a tough one." He thought for a moment. "Three weeks. Somewhere with a private beach, a lot of sun. Maybe Maui."

"Wedding?"

"Big."

"Ten-year anniversary gift?"

"Rae . . ."

"I'm curious."

"My wife would learn to play golf."

It was such a specific answer that Rae couldn't help but laugh. "You play?"

"Not yet. If I get married, I figure I'll learn."

"No more questions?" James asked after a moment.

"No."

He tugged her to a stop. They were in the shadows of a tall oak, moonlight flickering between the leaves. "Then I have a question for you."

Rae looked up at him.

"Can I kiss you?" he asked, seriously.

There was nothing she would like more. "I'm not so sure it would be a good idea," she found herself replying.

He linked his arms around her, bringing her close. "Just one kiss?"

She reluctantly nodded. She wanted to kiss him, to find out if it would be as special as she imagined it might be. She eased herself forward, her arms resting on his shoulders.

The kiss was gentle, soft, careful. It made her more vulnerable than she had been in two years. She was letting him inside her heart. It made her tremble under his hands.

He broke the kiss off before it could progress. "Kissing is going to be a problem."

"We could not do it again," she felt honor bound to offer. She was still trying to sort out the emotions, how much she had enjoyed that kiss.

He hugged her.

"Rationing. One kiss per date. We might survive."

She leaned against him and returned the hug. "Come over tomorrow."

They both laughed.

"Come on, lady. It's late. You've got to go to work in a few hours. It's time I took you home."

Rae reluctantly let him start them walking again. After they reached her town house, it took only a couple of minutes for the movie to be rewound, the dishes from dinner to be repacked.

Rae stood in the doorway after James stepped out onto the porch, the sack balanced in his hand.

"I'm not going to do more than simply say good-night," he cautioned, even as he stepped closer.

"That's wise," Rae agreed.

"Do you feel like the rug just got pulled out from under your feet?"

It was nice to know she wasn't the only one. . . . "Yanked out," she clarified.

"What do you want to do about it?"

He was so close she could touch his face if she only raised her hand. "Take it one day at a time," she replied softly, wisely.

He leaned down and gently kissed her cheek. "Good answer, Rae. You like sandwiches?"

She blinked at the change of subject. "Sure."

"I'll bring lunch tomorrow if you can get twenty minutes away. Your complex has a pond, ducks, and a park bench."

Her smile lit up her face. "Thanks."

He smiled back. His free hand gently stroked her cheek. "Tell me to go home, I'm in trouble here."

Her hands gently touched his shirt. She took a deep breath and pushed him a step away. "Go home."

He stepped back, made it two steps down the walk before he turned. "Rae?"

She hadn't moved, didn't have the strength or the will. "Yeah?"

"Sweet dreams."

Her face tensed.

"What?" He came partway back.

She forced her smile. "Nothing. I'll dream sweet dreams," she promised. "I'll see you tomorrow, James."

He hesitated. "Good night, then."

"Good night."

"The duck on the end looks annoyed."

Rae bit into the center of her sandwich, trying to keep the inch-high stack of condiments from falling off. She was near the end and it was becoming an adventure to eat. "You would be, too, if your wife was flirting with another guy," she remarked when she could speak again. "That's Bradley. His wife is the one in front flirting

203

with the mallard."

"You've got them all named."

She finished the sandwich. "The same ducks have been coming back here for years."

James shifted his arm across the back of the bench. Rae took advantage of the situation to lean her head back. "Thanks for lunch."

He smiled. "My pleasure."

"You look tired."

"You don't," he replied with a grin. "In fact, I would suggest you might have overdone the caffeine this morning. You're . . . perky."

She pushed him in the ribs with her free hand. "I'll give you 'perky.' And quit ducking my question."

He laughed at her pun.

"Ohh." She gave up and joined him, his laughter contagious.

"I didn't sleep because I was busy thinking," he told her when his laughter died down.

"Serious thinking?"

"Hmm. Got a question for you."

She rested a hand on his chest. "Oh, boy. Another question. Am I going to like it?"

He grinned. "Well, it took me several hours to phrase it, so you should."

She ducked her head against his chest. "Ask."

He rubbed her shoulders.

"You're not asking . . ." she said with a chuckle.

"Forgot the question. You're distracting, lady."

She sat back up, laughing. She hadn't felt this lighthearted in ages.

"I think we can safely say we are past the preliminaries in this dating adventure, wouldn't you agree?"

She thought about it carefully. "Yes," she said with a decisive nod.

He tickled her for that exaggeration. "Here's my question."

She was still laughing. She struggled to get serious. "Okay."

"This is a really important question," he reminded her, waiting until she nodded. "Will you . . ." He paused. "This is a really important question, Rae," he reminded her.

She tried to stifle the giggle. "Okay, okay. Ask."

"Rae, will you . . . help me pick out the wallpaper for the kitchen?"

She blinked at him. "Wallpaper."

He nodded, his expression serious. "Wallpaper."

She giggled. "I could probably do that."

"Will you help me hang it?"

"Only if you buy the brush-with-water kind. I'm dangerous with paste."

"Important point," he agreed. "Wallpaper with self-stick adhesive."

"I'm not very good at vertical stripes."

"I am," he replied smugly.

She was laughing so hard she was having a hard time catching her breath. "James, you spent last night thinking about your house?"

"I wouldn't want you to think I spent it just thinking about you."

"That wouldn't do," she agreed, solemnly.

She reluctantly checked her watch. "I've got to go back to work."

He gently brushed her hair back from her face. "Thanks for lunch."

She grinned. "I loved lunch."

"Come here," he whispered, tugging her toward him.

Her hands came to rest against his chest.

He kissed her, softly, gently. "Go back to work. Think about me occasionally."

She reluctantly got to her feet. "If I think about you, I won't get any work done."

He quirked one eyebrow with his smile. "Your concentration is that distractible?"

"I think I will plead the fifth," she replied with a smile, reluctantly slipping her hand from his. "See you later."

"I'm sure you will."

"Dave, the paint is suppose to be on the porch, not on me," Rae protested, tugging the sleeve of her shirt around to check out the latest white splotch.

"Sorry."

She gave a resigned sigh. "Sure you are."

There were footsteps behind them. "Aren't you two done yet?"

"Lace, you stuck me with someone who bites the tip of her tongue when she paints and who insists we leave no brush strokes visible anywhere. We are still going to be painting this porch next week."

Lace laughed and tweaked Dave's collar. "Did you know you've got a white handprint on your back?"

"Rae!"

She shrugged, even as she grinned. "Sorry."

"Would you two children like to come and eat? The pizza is here," James announced from the doorway. He and Kevin had been plastering the new wall they had built after tearing down two others.

Rae looked up from where she sat on the porch. "Sounds good to me."

"Feed her, James, please. She's driving me nuts."

James laughed and offered his hand to Rae, pulled her to her feet. "Hold it." He rescued her ponytail from shifting through the wet paint on her T-shirt. He tugged his baseball cap off and tucked her hair up in it. Grinned. "Okay, you're safe now."

"Dave should not be allowed to have a paintbrush."

James turned her around to inspect what had once been a pair of blue jeans and a hockey T-shirt. "Rae, you sat in wet paint?"

She glared at her friend. "He lied."

"I only said the step was going to need painting again. It did. You sat in it," Dave explained.

"I was naive this morning," Rae told James.

James tried to hide a smile. "Apparently."

"You're supposed to be on my side," she protested, seeing the smile.

He leaned down and kissed her paint-freckled nose. "I am." He tugged her hand. "Come on, let's eat."

Rae sat beside James on the backyard deck sharing pizza off his plate, sitting as close to him as she could get on the stoop. It had been nice, spending the last three weeks dating him. If she had to put it in one word, the last three weeks had been . . . *fun. Wonderful* was a good word. Or maybe the word she should choose would be *cautious*. No. Neither one of them were being cautious, per se, they both knew where they were heading, though they were taking their time.

One of these days she was going to admit to herself she was falling in love again. One of these days . . .

"I'm glad you came."

Rae smiled. "So am I." She lifted his soda can.

"Rae —" Lace pushed open the patio door "— come settle this debate. Dave insists I've got this striped wallpaper upside down. It doesn't have an up or down."

James smiled. "Go." He watched Rae head inside to settle the debate between her friends. He loved being around them, their laughter and their jokes, their teasing. A day with all of them meant a lot of inevitable laughter.

He was in love with Rae. In the last three weeks, any doubt about that had been removed. He loved her. He loved the way she looked, the way she smiled, the way she moved, the way she liked to snuggle, her confidence, her willingness to look at something that needed to be done and not shirk back, her willingness to give of herself to her employees, her clients, her friends — even at a personal cost. James could understand now why Leo had been so firm about making sure Rae had time to work on her book. Rae would give herself away and leave no time for herself.

James finished the soda.

They had some major issues to sort out. She needed time to think through what she wanted to do about her work. He wished he could solve the dilemma, find her a partner, but after several long talks with Dave, he better understood the obstacles she was dealing with. He couldn't add the pressure of an engagement to what she was already struggling with.

A few more weeks of time. It was the best gift he could give her right now.

She was going to say yes. He could read that in her eyes when he kissed her.

She was going to make a wonderful wife.

He carefully rubbed his left wrist. He was back to about an eight on his ten-point scale. A few more days, and even the stiffness should be gone.

He owed Rae some dance lessons.

"Rae, are you sure I can't get you something? A sandwich? A bagel?"

Rae shifted from where she was stretched

out on Lace's couch, turned to look over at her friend. "Thanks, Lace, but really, I'm fine."

It was a quarter past eight on a Thursday night. At the office, Rae had looked at the clock, decided enough was enough, and tossed the work into her briefcase. The briefcase was sitting in the front seat of her car now, would eventually get opened. The conference call was for 7:00 a.m. She still had eleven hours to get the work done, get some sleep. She would manage. "I like your dog." The little dog was curled up on Rae's chest, loving the attention.

"It looks like Tiger likes you, as well." Lace sat down in the chair. "You need to get a dog."

"Someday," Rae agreed. "What time is your flight to New York?"

"Six a.m. I'm on the return flight at two."

"That means you will get to see the airport, the inside of a cab, and the law offices of Glitchard, Pratt and Walford."

"Basically."

Rae struggled to hold a yawn back. Lying down was reinforcing how tired she was. Work was under control for a change, but it was costing her a lot of sleep.

"Rae, are you really thinking about getting married?"

The question caught Rae off guard. "Why do you say that?"

"Little things. The way you smile when you're with James."

Rae bit her bottom lip. "I've been thinking about it," she finally admitted. "It's scary, Lace. I let Leo get so close, and then I lost him. What if something happens to James?"

"Are you really worried about that? Losing James?"

"I don't know. It's not like I think he will die in an accident like Leo did. It's more my cautious side putting up a reason to not let the relationship go any further."

They both grew quiet.

"I don't know if I could handle getting married. It changes your life so much," Lace finally said.

"I don't mind being single, but I've been single for a long time. I'm ready to change that. I still want kids, Lace."

Lace smiled. "A Sunday morning in the nursery makes that pretty clear. You're right. It's one thing to be single for ten years. It's another to think about being single for your lifetime." Lace slid over a footstool. "James will make a good husband, Rae."

Rae moved the dog so he would not

tumble off. "Probably. I don't know if I'm as cut out to be a wife though."

"What bothers you about being a wife?"

"His expectations. Leo knew me before he fell in love with me. He knew the reality of who I was and who I was never going to be. James — I'm worried that he sees what he wants to see. You know me, Lace. You know how focused I get at work. You know what I think about decorating, and keeping house and cooking. I'm worried about the little things that James doesn't consider a problem now being a big deal after we have been married five years."

"You have to learn how to be married. You both will. I'm sure there are things about James that will bug you the same way in five years."

"Really? What? That's my problem. The guy is too perfect. He likes his mom. He's reliable, honest, kind. He knows where he is going. He is good at his job. He thinks for himself. It's kind of scary."

Lace laughed. "Oh, Rae. You have got it bad."

"Change the subject. I'm getting nervous just thinking about it. Can you imagine what the first week of the marriage would be like? What every meal would be like?"

"Let him teach you to cook. In five years,

you should have the basics down."

Rae grimaced. "Thanks a lot, friend."

"Have you decided what you are going to wear tomorrow night for our night out with the guys?"

Dave and James were taking them out for dinner, then dancing. "No. What are you going to wear?"

"Probably the blue silk. Why don't you wear the black dress? I'll loan you my short black velvet jacket."

"It is a beautiful dress." It was one of her favorite outfits.

"Dave made dinner reservations for seven-thirty?"

"Yes. Will you have time to get ready, given your flight schedule?"

"As long as the flight is not delayed, I'll be fine."

James was early.

Rae hurried to gather her clutch purse and shoes, carried them with her as she went downstairs.

"We should have done this a long time ago," James finally said after a slow appraisal of her, his expression one of frank appreciation.

Rae couldn't control the blush. She stepped back as he came inside. "I'm glad you like it," she replied, smiling, trying to keep her voice light. She had never been very good at the emotional interplay and she was on uncomfortable ground, immensely glad he appreciated her appearance, at the same time flustered by the frank attention.

James reached out and caught her hand, drew her toward him. "I think . . ."

When he didn't finish his sentence, she looked up. His eyes were studying her face, waiting for that movement. He smiled, his hand reaching up to caress her cheek. ". . . that we should start this evening with a kiss."

She suddenly grinned.

She liked being close to him. She could see the laughter and the love in his eyes. It was okay to be a little nervous. It didn't last. She stepped forward a little so she could lean against him. "Do you really?" she asked, tilting her head back to watch him.

His hands locked behind her waist. "I do."

She paused to consider the offer. "I like the idea. . . ."

He smiled. "But?"

"It's going to be really hard to keep my mind on dinner and dancing if every time I look at you tonight, I'm remembering this kiss," she replied, answering his smile.

"I can fix that."

"Really?"

He nodded. "Close your eyes."

She giggled; she couldn't help it. "James."

"I'm not letting you go until I get this kiss," he remarked.

Rae thought about it and quietly closed her eyes. She could feel him lean down. Ready for the kiss, she held perfectly still . . . and the kiss didn't come.

She opened her eyelashes a fraction.

He was waiting for her to do just that. He smiled and swiftly kissed her. She loved this man so much.

His forehead rested against hers. "We need to go eat." His voice was reluctant.

"Hmm." Rae sighed and slowly stepped back, knowing he was right.

James tweaked a lock of her hair. "Do you have a wrap? It's chilly tonight."

Rae stepped into the living room where she had a coat that went with the dress.

James held it for her as she slipped it on.

His attention to the details, locking the door for her, walking beside her to the car, holding her door for her, were noticed and appreciated. He did it naturally, and the attention meant a great deal to Rae.

"Where did you and Dave decide on for dinner?"

"Tobias House. It is quiet, elegant, but still has a really good steak."

Rae chuckled. "Okay. I can tell where your priorities are."

"I was working on the upstairs guest room today, I'm ready for a good meal."

"You got the window replaced?"

"Just about. Since we had to open up the wall already to put in the larger window, we decided to go ahead and move some of the electrical wiring, put in more insulation. Another day, and the guest room will be finished."

"The house is almost done."

James smiled. "Just needs a woman's decorative touch," he agreed.

Rae decided not to touch that comment. They were heading somewhere; she just wasn't sure how ready she was for the next step. It was hard enough admitting to herself how deeply she had fallen in love with him. That knowledge should be filling her with joy. It was, but it also felt a little scary.

James reached over and gently touched the bottom lip she was biting. "Don't. We've got all the time in the world, Rae. I'm not suggesting anything."

She stopped the unconscious gesture. "I

know, James. It just feels really big sometimes, this relationship."

He clicked on the right turn signal. "I know what you mean. It's scary from my side, too."

She turned to look at him, surprised. "Really?"

"Really. I got a surprise with you, Rae. I wasn't expecting to come back to the States to stay, let alone find you. I like to plan my life, and I wasn't planning this."

Rae leaned her head against the seat headrest and smiled. "We're even, then. I wasn't expecting to meet you, either."

James laughed, reached over to pull her hand into his. "Don't get me wrong, Rae. Now that I've found you, I have no intention of letting you go."

"I think that's one of the sweetest things you've ever said to me."

He raised their linked hands and kissed the back of her wrist. "Just don't tell Dave that, he already thinks I'm way too mushy. Lace wants him to follow suit."

Rae laughed. "I'm sure he told you to be on your best behavior tonight, didn't he?"

"Why do you think I wanted to get the kiss in before we joined them?"

Dave and Lace had not yet arrived at the

restaurant, so James and Rae requested their table and went on in to be seated.

The restaurant had subdued lighting, white linen tablecloths, romantic music. "I can't believe I've never been here before," Rae remarked, accepting the cloth-covered menu.

"It is a really nice place," James agreed, glancing around.

They agreed on an appetizer plate, went ahead and ordered soft drinks.

"How is Patricia doing?"

"Fine. Eager to have a baby in the house again. She started decorating the nursery this last week."

"She's feeling okay?"

James nodded. "Seems to be. She's still very active."

"Are you looking forward to having another niece or nephew?"

"Definitely. I used to baby-sit Emily."

"You did?"

"I like that stage where they are just learning to walk. Every day you would get surprised with the latest hurdle they had mastered. One day she couldn't walk, and the next day, there she is, on her feet and wobbling across the room. It was great."

"I like that age with the kids in the nursery, too. They change from being infants to toddlers almost overnight."

Dave and Lace arrived with apologies for being late, and the conversation shifted to greetings. They looked adorable as a couple, Rae decided, watching as Dave held the chair for Lace, leaned down to whisper something to her. Lace looked flushed, the apologies had been a little overblown. They had probably been stealing a couple moments together before coming into the restaurant. James had apparently reached the same conclusion, because his greetings to Dave were accompanied by a slightly raised eyebrow.

Dave sat down beside Lace. "We got detained," he said simply, choosing not to go further. "Have you already ordered?"

A trip to the ladies' room would have to be engineered, Rae decided. Lace was in love. It had her confused, and off balance, but Lace was most certainly in love.

Rae took pity on her and ensured the next ten minutes of conversation were focused on Dave and how the case he was defending was coming along. It put the evening back on the normal casual friendship tone for all of them. They ate dinner talking, laughing together, as four old friends, not as two couples.

It had been a wise move to make. When

dinner reached the dessert stage, Rae felt as if she had finally relaxed. She caught James watching her a few times during the meal, shared a private smile with him, but otherwise the tone stayed in neutral territory.

It was Lace who suggested where they should go dancing, a club that was known for its good blues. The place was typically busy, but not packed on a Friday night. Her suggestion was readily adopted.

Rae indicated she was going to stop at the ladies' room before they left and Lace joined her.

They were fixing their makeup when Rae finally decided to broach the subject. "What happened before dinner?"

"He wants me to go with him to a dinner party being hosted by one of the firm's senior partners."

"That's big."

"That's huge. They don't like the idea of having a senior partner who is single. That's the only reason they are throwing the party, to see who Dave will shake out of the woodwork to bring."

Rae understood. Lace didn't like being considered a solution to Dave's problem. Rae was blotting her lipstick when she had a brilliant idea. "Why don't you accept that job offer from Olsen, Richmond, and

Quinn? There is no way Dave would take the member of a rival firm to a party thrown by a senior partner unless he cared more about you than he did about what the other senior partners thought."

Lace paused, touching up her blush. "That would be devious and underhanded." She was smiling even as she said it. "I couldn't do that."

Rae picked up her clutch bag. "I know you couldn't. You're in love. But the thought does makes the situation seem more palatable."

Lace chuckled. "I think I'll be more direct. It will cost him that watercolor painting I found at the gallery last week."

"Bribery works well," Rae agreed, smiling. Her friend looked good, being in love. It made her eyes glow. Rae wondered if she had the same expression, hoped hers was a little more contained. "Are you glad you came tonight?"

Lace smiled. "Yes. I like having Dave know he has to act like a gentleman. He even brought me flowers."

James made a point of taking hold of Rae's hand when they reached the club. They walked across the parking lot to join Dave and Lace. He liked holding her hand.

She was his date, and he didn't intend to leave that to anyone's interpretation. She willingly interlaced her fingers with his.

Dave had his arm around Lace's waist.

As they opened the door to the club, the music drifted out into the night. Stepping inside was like entering a contained world, the music, the lights, the large group of people, most on the dance floor, some sitting at tables grouped along the walls.

They checked the ladies' coats, and Dave scanned the room for a table. "Over here."

James kept his hand on the small of Rae's back as they followed Dave and Lace through the crowd. It was a beautiful room, decorated in cherry wood, polished gold fixtures, and an abundance of greenery. The tables were packed close together and they stepped to the side several times as waitresses and other guests moved through the same small aisle.

Dave had found a table on the raised-floor platform, near the band. James held Rae's chair as she took her seat, let his hands gently squeeze her shoulders before pulling out the chair beside her.

"Would anyone like something to drink?" Dave asked, catching the eye of a waitress.

"A ginger ale," Lace requested, scanning the room to see if she knew anyone present.

"Diet soda," Rae replied.

"Make it two," James agreed. "Rae, shall we check out the dance floor?" They could sit and talk or they could dance. James would prefer to dance. She had gone tense as they walked to the table; the fastest way to ease her apprehension was to show her she would do fine.

She wanted to decline, but he held out his hand, smiling, and she conceded, putting her hand in his. "Sure."

He had yet to figure out what perfume she was wearing, but he liked it. He liked it a lot. She had brushed her long hair back and secured it with a gold clasp, the pattern in the clasp shining under the lights as they walked down to the dance floor.

James paused at the edge of the floor, gently caught both her hands to turn her toward him. She had such a beautiful face. He thought about kissing her but instead simply smiled. "Why don't you show me what you know?"

His request made her smile, her eyes reflecting her laughter. Her hands rested softly on his shoulders. "I suppose that would be a good place to start," she agreed demurely.

James settled his hands on her waist with a smile. "Concentrate on where you place those high heels, Rae."

She chuckled. "Okay, teach me how to dance, I'll leave you alone."

James laughed and willingly moved them onto the dance floor.

She fit in his arms, followed his lead, obviously loved to dance, her problem was more a lack of confidence than skill. He solved that problem by keeping her totally distracted. They managed two songs before he couldn't resist leaning down to kiss her. "You are doing great."

He loved her smile.

They spent two hours at the club. It was an evening that James was reluctant to see come to an end, but eventually out of courtesy to Rae — he knew how long her week had been — he suggested they call it an evening.

Rae slipped off her shoes as she watched James's car pull out of her driveway. It had been hard to say good-night. She loved being with him, loved being near him. He had stopped at the front door, kissed her good-night, and quietly said thank-you for a wonderful evening. Rae had echoed his sentiments.

Church Sunday and the chance to sit with him was too far away.

She took off the velvet jacket and the dress with care. It had been the perfect choice for an outfit. She smiled as she took off her makeup. James had liked it.

She was tired, a deep tiredness that had settled on her as James drove her home. She longed for bed and the chance to sleep until her body decided to wake up.

Leo's picture on her nightstand made her pause. She picked it up, carefully slid off the ribbon and the ring. Her smile in the picture was of a woman in love. She had seen that smile again tonight, a few minutes ago, as she washed off her makeup. She was in love with James. The same kind of love she had felt for Leo.

Her finger gently traced over the glass.

She was ready to move on. The past was behind her.

She thought about it for a moment, then carried the picture with her to the drawer where she kept her mother's diaries, gently set Leo's picture there.

The ring. She closed her hand around it, feeling the cool metal, the beautiful diamond; she put the ring with her mother's wedding ring.

The past was closed.

Chapter Nine

"What's wrong?"

James instantly masked the pain. He hadn't heard Rae come back into the room. He had moved to get up from the plush couch and the pain in his hips and knees had brought tears to his eyes. "Nothing. I've been sitting too long," he said, dismissing whatever she had seen.

She handed him the drink she had brought for him. It was a sign of how hard her day had been that in the dim room she didn't realize he was lying. She dropped down on the couch beside him. He had only a few seconds warning to clench his jaw against the motion. What had seemed mild three hours ago had become agonizing pain now. It was so bad, even holding the glass of soda she had brought him hurt.

They were at Dave's, the movie paused yet again, this time while Dave answered a call. Rae had arrived late and had been interrupted by six pages during the past two hours. She rested beside him now, her head back, her eyes closed, and he could feel the weariness enveloping her. The weariness was one reason he was doing his best to shield her from what was happening again, the return of the pain.

"Go home and get some sleep, Rae. You don't need to be here." She looked as if she had barely slept in the last three days.

"Dave's got trust papers being delivered here tonight that I need for tomorrow," she replied, too weary to open her eyes. "I'm sorry, James. I'm lousy company tonight."

He gently brushed her hair back from her face. "Rae, quit apologizing for the markets tumbling. I know how hard you've been working lately."

"I've never lost so much money so fast in my life. Why Taiwan and China had to go at it this month, of all months . . ." She struggled to open her eyes. "If I sit here, I'm going to fall asleep, and then I'll be groggy for the drive home, and end up being a danger to everyone around me. Maybe Dave can bring the papers by my place in the morning."

"Of course I can," Dave agreed, coming back into the room. "Go home, Rae. And turn off the pager for six hours. You need some uninterrupted sleep."

She leveraged herself tiredly to her feet, her hand on James's arm, leaned over to quietly kiss him good-night. "Sorry," she whispered. "I need to get some sleep."

"Go. Drive carefully."

"It's two miles. I'll call when I get home."

He kissed her back, hating to see the exhaustion in her eyes. "I'll be waiting for the call."

Dave walked with her to the door, making arrangements for the morning.

James winced when Dave came back, turned the room lights back up. "Okay, what's going on? Rae put her hand on your arm for leverage and you went white as a sheet."

"Quit being a lawyer, Dave, and get me some aspirin."

He crossed the room. "Can you even get to your feet?"

James laughed, ironically. "Dave, I can't reach forward to set the glass down right now, my joints are so painful."

Dave pushed the coffee table back with his foot, took the glass. "What happened?"

James eased himself forward to the edge of the couch, sweat coursing down his forehead. "Something set it off, I don't know what. A virus, something. Three hours ago it was discomfort, now it's excruciating."

"Let's get you to the hospital."

James shook his head. "Get me the phone, and that cane you loaned me once before. I know this routine by heart. Whatever the doctor is going to prescribe, I've already got at home."

It was agonizing waking up. Agonizing to breathe. Every breath forced his chest muscles to expand, every breath meant pain.

The doorbell had woke him up. He was on the couch. Apart from the fact that the painkillers the doctor prescribed had stopped him in his tracks last night, the stairs were something he had no plans to climb anytime soon.

It took him a very, very long time to walk from the living room to the front door.

Rae.

There was sweat from his journey marking his forehead, and nothing could disguise the white, taut jaw; he was enduring the pain and it showed.

He saw tears fill her eyes.

"You should have told me."

He had to smile. He had known her response would be this, but still, knowing it was not the same as experiencing it. It mattered a great deal that she was here, at his place, to check on him in person. She wasn't at the end of the phone, or at work where she rightfully needed to be right now. "Rae, I'm fine. Go on to work."

"You always answer the door walking with a cane?"

He leaned against the doorjamb, easing the pain in his spine by finding a solid support to take some of his weight, wanting to invite her inside, but not wanting to endure the walk down the hall.

"I'm sorry. I should have told you. Or at least called you this morning."

She reached out her hand to touch him, uncertainty making her hesitate before she very gently rested her hand against his forearm. "I am so sorry you're in pain again."

She was. It made him ache, knowing he had added to the load she was carrying. He hated the malicious randomness of this disease. "Come here," James said quietly, reaching for her hand. He drew her a couple steps closer to him. It was difficult, looking at the strain she carried from several nights without sleep, knowing he had added to the weight she carried, seeing the tears. He loved her. He didn't want to cause this.

He wiped away her tears, then very carefully leaned down to kiss her. "Go on, Rae. I can maneuver around just fine, if a little slower than normal. Go to work. It's nothing new, nothing I haven't dealt with before. It's the same symptoms, the same disease. I will be okay. Come tonight and crash on my couch and see for yourself I'm really going to be okay."

"You'll need someone to carry things for you, fix you lunch . . ."

He grinned.

"Okay, maybe not fix you lunch . . . but answer the phone, answer the door. I should be here."

His fingers gently silenced her. "You need to be at work. I need those things to keep me fighting the pain, working to defeat it. Go do what you have to do today, call me occasionally, and when you are honestly finished, not before, come back and keep me company." He smiled. "I'm not going anywhere today."

She bit her lip.

"Rae, I promise. I won't keep any more surprises from you."

"Is this what a day you would score a one looks like?"

James hesitated. "This is a two, Rae. You'll know one when you see it."

"I hope I never do."

"I hope that, too." It would scare the daylights out of you if you did. . . .

"Will you page me if you need anything? Anything at all?"

"I will," he promised softly. "Go to work, beautiful."

She had elected to sit in a chair rather than beside him on the couch. He was exhausted to the point of wanting to collapse, but he didn't have the heart to tell her to go home. It was seven o'clock and she had arrived only a short time before.

Trust the illness to rob him of even a hug from her. He hated this unnamed disease, he hated it tremendously.

She knew. "I should go, you're tired."

"No," James protested, so that she hesitated as she rose from her seat. "You haven't told me how your day went yet," he encouraged.

He could do so little for her, the one thing he could offer was a willingness to listen.

"You don't need more bad news and I don't want to think about it."

"Tell me. If you don't, you'll be replaying the day in your dreams."

Rae sighed. "The total market was down another two percent today. That makes eight percent this week, twelve percent in the last seven trading days. Even companies I thought of as stable are in trouble. And clients are calling, feeling the need to make changes, forcing me to sell positions I would normally have allowed to ride out the correction. A broker got shot today in New York by a client holding big option positions he was going to be forced to cover. It's becoming that kind of a panic."

"Are you holding up, Rae?"

"It's a walk in the park compared to what you're dealing with."

"Oh, I don't know. At least I can clear my schedule to deal with this. Have you been able to clear your weekend to give yourself time to sleep?"

"James, I want to be here. I'll sleep in, then come over."

"Not before noon. You need the sleep, Rae."

She reluctantly nodded. "Noon. I'll stop somewhere and bring us lunch."

Saturday came. Four days and the pain was still excruciating. James shaved, having to pause frequently because his hand could not grip the razor. He hurt. Every joint, every muscle. He looked in the mirror and hated the fatigue, the pain. He had not been able to sleep, the pain was too intense, and his face showed it. Rae did not need to see him like this.

He could hear his mom downstairs, moving around in the kitchen.

He turned on the faucet, suppressing the pain from his wrists. It was wearing him down. Wearing down his ability to be optimistic about anything. How many times was he going to have to endure flare-ups like this? Each time it happened, his body took longer to recover. Longer to heal.

Was this the time he simply wasn't going to recover?

He forced himself to move, to ignore the question.

He was not going to let fatigue rob him of his optimism; he was going to recover, he had done it before, and he would do it again. Small step, by small step. He had made it upstairs today.

It was progress. He smiled wryly. Just as long as he didn't fall down the stairs going down.

He was tired of this. Tired of being tired. Tired of being in pain.

It was the last thing he wanted Rae to see.

God, why this? Why now? I don't understand.

He was sitting at the kitchen table, glancing at the paper, eating an iced cinnamon roll his mom had recently taken from the oven, when the doorbell rang. James looked at the cane. His body protested at the thought.

"I'll get it," his mom called from the living room. She had been cleaning his house again even though he had a cleaning service that came in each week. James had realized his mom was going to do what she decided to do and nothing would stop her. He had kissed her cheek and let her go to it. He was grateful for the love behind it.

He knew it was Rae. He had told her to come over no earlier than noon and it was now five minutes past the hour. He got to his feet as she entered into the room, ignoring her "Don't get up." She had slept in, but not enough for what her body desperately needed. She looked . . . wiped out.

"How are you?" she asked, stopping close to him, her eyes searching his face.

He leaned forward to gently kiss her. "Better now that you're here." He meant it, even if his body ached at the movement.

"Rae, would you like some coffee?" his mom asked. "I've got homemade cinnamon rolls, too. Fresh from the oven."

Rae pulled out a chair beside James at the table. "Both sound wonderful. Thank you."

James sat down carefully.

"You didn't get much sleep," Rae said softly.

James smiled. "Not much. But I don't think you did, either."

She grimaced. "No."

He motioned to the paper. "It sounds like the markets finally had a quiet day yesterday."

Rae nodded. "Probably the prelude to a bad Monday. There is concern the economic numbers being released Monday morning will prompt a rise in interest rates."

He studied her face and saw in her eyes the fatigue that went too deep to cover, the exhaustion that made dealing with decisions so difficult you reached the point it didn't matter anymore. She may have slept in, but stopping had just let the fatigue crash down on her. She ought to be back in bed, sleeping away the entire day.

He hated this disease. She needed someone taking care of her, not the other way around.

His mom brought coffee and the cinnamon rolls, then left them to talk. A few minutes later, James heard vacuuming upstairs.

Rae ate the cinnamon roll slowly, trying to get a conversation started, trying to inject some emotion into her voice, but the exhaustion was too heavy. She would lose her train of thought and go quiet for increasing amounts of time. Just sitting down had made her body long to sleep.

James pushed himself carefully to his feet, his ankles flaring with pain at the movement. He clenched his jaw and ignored the pain. "Rae, come on. The living room couch beckons."

She moved with him to the other room. He lowered himself down on the couch, using the armrest to keep the movement slow.

Rae moved toward the chair and James stopped her. "Sit beside me Rae, please."

She was reluctant to do so, but he didn't release her hand and didn't give her much choice. She sat down on the couch beside him. He wanted her to rest, put her head against his shoulder and close her eyes, but she protested she was fine, just a little tired. He looked at her skeptically.

She reached for the television remote. "Which college teams are playing today?"

Discussions of a serious nature were not going to happen today. James reluctantly let the conversation change to basketball.

His ribs hurt where her weight leaned against him. She had been farther away on the couch and he had intentionally maneuvered her closer so she leaned against him and he could put his arm around her. It took twenty minutes, but the pain won the contest of wills. He was at the point of having to ask her to shift away from him when he saw her try to unsuccessfully stifle a yawn. He pulled a couple of throw pillows over. "Rae, stretch out on the couch and get comfortable. I won't mind if you catnap for a while."

She turned to look up at him. He could see the fatigue shadowing her eyes. "You don't mind?"

He tenderly brushed her cheek with his hand. "I don't mind," he reassured softly. "Come on, stretch out."

She moved away from him and the pain in his ribs began to ease. Her shoes landed on top of each other on the floor and she stretched out, using the pillows he offered to rest comfortably against the other end of the sofa. "Thank you, James."

"Close your eyes and try to get some more sleep," he whispered.

Within ten minutes he could hear her breathing become steady and low as she slept.

It felt good, it felt right, to have her relaxed with him. He muted the basketball game, then leaned his head back against the cushions, and watched her sleep.

They had to do something about the hours she was working. She couldn't keep up the pace, not when she was this exhausted.

"Rae, I understand. Don't worry about it. Go meet with the clients then call me when you get home."

He was going to miss not having dinner with her, but it was probably best today that her work had intruded. He was stretched out in the recliner, looking at the bird that had come to check out the bird feeder, waiting for the medication to temper the ache in his body. It had been fourteen days since the relapse began, and even the careful exercises in the pool each day were agonizing. The doctors had come up with nothing that could even check the damage. His joints were inflamed, his muscles burning. He lost more and more mobility each day.

Dave knew, but with Rae it was a carefully laid out cover-up. She was worried enough about him that it was important to try to hide the worst from her.

He had watched her over the past two weeks, moving toward the point of being close to collapse herself. She was not getting the sleep she needed. She was worried about him, trying to make time in her schedule to come over and help him, doing it at the expense of her sleep.

He hated the situation. He hated it with a passion.

He wanted to be well. He wanted to be able to be the one to go to her place, fix dinner for her, take care of errands for her, help ease the pressure on her. Instead, this disease was ensuring he was adding to the stress she was feeling.

He spent the evening reading a book, often pausing to set the book aside, to lean his head back, think, pray.

If he didn't begin to recover soon, he wasn't sure what he was going to do. But he couldn't do this to Rae. He couldn't let this disease end up affecting her health as well. He refused to let that happen.

It was a quarter to eleven at night when Rae rang Dave's doorbell. He came down the steps from his studio office, flipped on the porch light. He saw her and flipped the locks open. He was still in sweats from an evening playing basketball at the gym.

She didn't apologize for the hour. Their history went back many years. He knew, without being told. He took her jacket and draped it over the stair railing, then put his arm around her as he walked her to the kitchen.

"You look . . . tired, my friend."

She took the soda he offered. "You understate things very well." She took a long drink. "Can you get me tickets to San Diego for tomorrow morning, return flight Sunday night? Lunch and dinner reservations at a quiet, elegant place conducive to talking serious business?"

He looked at her and she let him see the truth, let her mask slip to show the reality going on.

"I'll be glad to Rae. Find a comfortable spot on the couch, relax. I'll make a few calls."

He joined her in the living room twenty minutes later, handed her a piece of paper from his desk stationery.

Rae glanced at it wearily, knowing it would be complete, finding it was. A limo to pick her up from the office, first-class seats there and back, restaurant reservations, hotel accommodations, Dave had arranged it all, or rather one of his contacts had. "Thank you," she said softly.

He handed her two business cards. "They are good. Use them if you need them."

Two attorneys, both top names in the business. Men you didn't just make appointments with; they picked their clients.

"The numbers are their direct lines. They will make themselves available."

Rae nodded, knowing it would be true. "Thanks, friend."

"You're going to sell."

She leaned her head back against the cushion, looked at the ceiling. "I'm going to . . . consider the possibilities. The Hamilton trusts are not definite, but the indications from dinner tonight are positive. I've got to have help, Dave. Good help. Since I can't find the right partner with the business at twenty-six million, I'm going to do my best to make it a business of seventy million and see if I can get either Richardson in Texas or Walters in New York to move. They are the only two men whose track records and style fit what I really need. But if neither one of them works out —" she sighed as she looked at the page of notes "— then yes, I'm seriously considering selling the business."

Dave rubbed her hand which was clenching and unclenching around the throw pillow she had picked up. "Rae, Gary is a good guy. He'll make you a fair offer, he'll keep your employees, he'll do good for your clients. There could be worse solutions."

She heard the reluctance in his voice. "You don't think I should sell."

"I think you're going to really miss the work."

She sighed and looked at the page of notes again. "I know. I've told myself for months that I would do it only as my literal last resort. But I'm close to being there, friend."

"You're tired."

She laughed. "I can barely remember the last day I felt rested. I don't want this anymore, Dave. I don't want the responsibility and the fatigue and the hours. I'll find a partner, or I'll face the reality and sell."

James touched the tile wall of the pool, let himself finally stop. Five laps. It wasn't great, it was a long, long way from fifty laps, but it meant he was finally back to a four on his scale of pain. He let the water float his body as he tried to catch his breath. A month. It felt like an eternity.

He had begun to privately wonder if the recovery was ever going to come. It was a battle to keep hope alive and at the same time try to accept and live with reality.

He would take Rae to dinner tonight to celebrate.

The idea brought a smile. She had been traveling on weekends this past month —

San Diego, Texas, New York — business meetings with outcomes she remained non-committal about. He had missed her, missed the Saturday afternoons spent together, the rare chance to see her without the burden of work pressing on her.

The past month had simply reinforced how important she had become in his life. It was one of the reasons he had struggled so hard to keep hope alive. If he didn't recover, they didn't have a future together. That reality had made him willing to push through the pain and endure the toll the exercises took. There was finally a glimmer of hope, and it was time to celebrate.

Rae's office was less than twenty minutes away. He felt like making the request in person.

Janet pointed him toward the trading room with a smile.

"Hey, lady," he called softly, pausing at the door to watch Rae. Her attention was so focused on the information in front of her, his words startled her.

"James!"

He loved the sight of the smile that lit her face. She was glad to see him and it made him very glad he had come.

She crossed the room to join him at the

door. "What are you doing here?"

He leaned forward and softly kissed her, watched the blush spread across her cheeks. "Want to go out to dinner?"

"I would love to."

"When should I come back and pick you up?"

She looked back at the screen she had been studying, bit her bottom lip. "Give me twenty minutes and I can wrap this up for the night."

"You're sure? Don't hurry on my account."

She grinned. "Twenty minutes. Can we do Chinese?"

He laughed. "Yes."

They ate at the restaurant across from the office complex, a leisurely dinner, the conversation moving from Dave and Lace, to church, to her work.

She was close to signing a major new client and as he listened to her he heard the excitement, but inside he wondered if it was a good decision for her to make. A new client would increase her workload, increase the demands. He didn't understand entirely why the idea appealed so much to her. But it did, and he was not one to limit anyone's dreams — certainly not Rae's. It mattered to her, so it mattered to him.

He had been about a week premature in his decision to celebrate. By the end of the dinner, he was reluctantly ready to admit it was time to go home and rest. The pain was back, strong and fierce, ugly.

"Come on in, Rae. The door is open."

It was easier to call than to walk. His ankles were protesting even this journey to the kitchen. The hint of a recovery had been more of a wisp of hope than reality. Six weeks, and the pain in his joints was still severe.

The room vibrated to life with her entrance. Her eyes were sparkling and her cheeks were pink. "James, I got the contract. I'm going to be managing the Hamilton estate, and all its various trust funds."

"Rae, that's great," James said, pleased for her. He handed her one of the sodas he had retrieved. She accepted it from him with a thank-you and spontaneously reached forward to hug him.

She pulled back. "What kind of pizza . . . ?"

He hadn't been able to mask the pain in time.

She took a hesitant step back and her eyes suddenly widened.

"It hurts when I hug you," she said, the

appalling realization shaking her voice. "Oh, James. I'm sorry. I didn't think . . ."

He saw the look of horror fill her face, and then she turned abruptly and hurried from the room. He didn't have the luxury of being able to hurry after her. By the time he reached the door she had fled through, her car was already pulling from the drive.

Rae opened the door for him, her eyes red, her face pale. She looked at him and he looked just as seriously back at her. "Can we talk?" he finally asked.

She swung open the door and walked toward the living room.

James set his wallet and car keys down on the end table. She had moved to stand by the window, her arms wrapped around her middle. He stopped by the end of the couch and looked at her. It was better if she spoke first. It was a long wait.

"I wish you would just say when something causes you pain."

She was trying so hard not to cry. . . .

With a deep sigh, James crossed over to her side. He had never intended this.

She didn't want to look at him.

He tipped her chin up. "It hurts when you hug me, but I'm not going to let a little pain rob me of the pleasure. I love it when you hug me. I don't want you stopping to think before you hug me. That's why I didn't tell you."

He wiped away her tears. "Rae, I like your hugs."

It took several moments before she replied. "You're sure?"

"Absolutely."

She carefully wrapped her arms around him. "It feels so awful to realize I was hurting you."

He gently brushed her hair back from her face, settled his arms firmly around her waist. "Rae, it would hurt me worse to have you stop."

He held her for a long time, relieved to have her back.

He leaned down and gently kissed her. "Are we okay now?"

She sniffed a final time and nodded.

"Good. Then how about going out for that pizza?"

It made her laugh.

"Uncle James, I helped make the rolls. They are really good." His niece met him at the door, sliding her hand in his, smiling. James propped the cane in the umbrella stand. He thought he could get by without it today.

"That's great, Emily. You're going to become a great cook like your grand-mother."

"She made clam chowder. Do you like it?"

"Love it."

Emily's grin widened. "So do I. We've got turkey and dressing, and my rolls, scalloped potatoes — my mom made those — that green stuff I like, homemade noodles, and for dessert there's pumpkin pie, apple pie and chocolate pudding. I can't wait for lunch."

James laughed and tickled her tummy. "Where are you going to put all that food?" He wished he could pick her up. He knew better than to try.

"In my hollow leg," Emily replied, gig-gling.

James loved Thanksgiving Day. It was something they didn't celebrate in Africa.

"Where's your dad?"

"Getting the card tables from the base-ment."

The kitchen was busy, both his mom and sister fixing snack and relish trays. "Do you think we have enough to eat?" James asked, looking over the loaded counters.

His mom grinned and gently hugged him. "Even with nine people at the table, we're going to be sending lots of leftovers home with people. It's one of the things that makes it a good day. Are Dave and Lace with you?"

"They're on the way," James assured her. "They were going to go spring Rae from her office."

"She's working? Today?"

James grimaced. That was what he thought as well. "A couple of hours. Need any help?"

"We're close to being done."

James nodded. "Patricia, how's my future niece or nephew doing?" She was due in another eight weeks. His sister was loving being pregnant.

"Having a wonderful time kicking the inside of my ribs. He's an active little guy."

"Think it's a boy?"

Patricia grinned. "I've got a fifty-fifty chance of being right."

James affectionately squeezed her shoulder. "I pick New Years Day as the estimated time of arrival. I think you're going to be early."

Patricia laughed. "That would be fine with me."

James accepted a drink and went to see if he could help Paul. He couldn't carry much, but there should be something he could do. Find out what football games were on that afternoon if nothing else.

He was looking forward to seeing Rae. Dave and Lace, too.

He was having a moderately good day. A four on his scale of ten. He could walk without much pain today. It was probably a short reprieve, but he would take it while it lasted.

Dave, Lace and Rae arrived, amidst a lot of laughter. James met them at the door, grinned at Rae who was wearing a feather tucked in her hair.

"James, they are calling me a turkey."

"Gee, I wonder why."

She swatted his arm. "I have to show some Thanksgiving Day spirit. They wouldn't let me bring any food."

"Thank you both," James gratefully told Dave and Lace, then double-checked to make sure Rae knew he was teasing. He would hate to hurt her feelings. She wasn't *that* bad of a cook.

She tucked her hand under his arm. "One of these days, you are all going to regret these comments." She was grinning.

"Sure, sure. That's what you always say," Dave replied, grinning back.

"What did you bring?" James asked Lace, looking at the foil-covered tray she was carrying.

"Homemade candy. Fudge, chocolate-covered cherries, caramels."

"You've been hiding this talent all these months?"

Rae laughed. "Dave made them, James. Lace just sat on the stool and kept him company."

"I'm impressed," James told Dave.

"You should be. Caramels take forever to make."

They already knew everyone in his family, but Dave and Lace had not seen the house before, so James gave them a guided tour, not letting Rae get far from his side. She didn't seem to be in any hurry to move away either. His arm around her shoulders, he hugged her gently. He was very glad to have her here.

The kitchen timer went off, and Emily announced her rolls were done. It was time to eat.

Dave and Lace were flirting with each other. James watched the two of them as they moved around the buffet table filling their plates. Dave would lean over occasionally and make a soft comment; Lace would blush and whisper something back that would make Dave chuckle.

Rae nudged his arm. "They went to some comedy club downtown last night. I think

Lace had a good time," she whispered.

"I think you're right."

James held out the chair beside him at the table for Rae.

"Thanks."

"My pleasure."

Rae leaned against him as she asked if he would pass the butter.

James reached around her to pass the basket of rolls to Dave, let his arm linger around her shoulders.

"Would you two quit flirting and eat?" Patricia finally asked, laughing.

James and Rae looked over, caught, only to find that Patricia was looking at Dave and Lace.

"It goes for you, too, James," his mom said, seeing his look of relief.

"Me? I'm the innocent party in all this," James protested. Rae reached over and ruffled his hair.

He caught her hand, leaned over. He kissed her to the delight of those at the table. "If I'm going to get caught, it should be worth it," he told Rae softly, watching her blush.

She leaned forward until they were touching noses. "You just used up your one kiss for this date," she reminded him.

James blinked. She was right.

She laughed at his expression.

★ ★ ★

James took Rae home shortly after 9:00 p.m.

His mom had sent a sack of leftovers home with her — soup, sandwiches, noodles, pie. James reached for the sack on the back seat only to have Rae stop him. "Let me carry it."

"Rae . . ."

"I know it's a good day, I know it's not heavy. Humor me."

James was in too good a mood to argue the point. They walked up the drive together.

"What would you like to do tomorrow?"

"Sleep in till eight, have a leisurely breakfast, shop, go see a movie."

"Sounds perfect. I'll pick you up at eight-thirty?"

"That was only a suggestion, James. Are you sure you want to go shopping? It will be crazy tomorrow with the Thanksgiving Day sales and the start of the Christmas shopping."

"Shopping will be fun," he replied. "We've never done it together before."

Rae grinned. "There is a reason for that, you know."

James grinned back. "I'll take my chances. Eight-thirty?"

"Fine."

James leaned forward. "Can we make it a two kiss date?"

Rae moved the sack to her far arm. "I think that can be arranged," she replied with a smile. He leaned down to kiss her and Rae closed her eyes.

A groan of pain broke apart the kiss.

She had stepped forward. His left ankle refused to take his shifted weight. His reflex to keep from falling put his hand heavily on her shoulder.

"What . . . ?"

"I'm okay." He gingerly tried to put weight on the ankle. The tendons and joint flared with pain.

"I did it again." Rae was angry with herself, her arm going around his waist, the sack she still held tipping precariously. "James, I am so *sorry*."

"It's not your fault." He took several deep breaths, fighting back the pain. "It's why I carry the cane." The cane was, of course, still propped in the back seat of the car.

"I'll get it."

He stopped her movement. "No. Walk me back to the car. I've been on my feet too long today."

It was a painfully ugly way to end the evening.

Rae walked with him back to the car,

James clenching his teeth at the pain in his left ankle. If it had been his right, Rae would have been driving him home. "We'll have to play tomorrow by ear," he said, admitting the obvious.

"No problem, it's not important. Call me when you get up."

It *was* important and it *was* a big deal. But he didn't have a lot of options.

"I'll call you," he agreed, resigned. The pain had managed to ruin a good evening.

The phone rang at eight-thirty the next morning.

"Did I wake you up?"

Rae smiled. "No. Though I am still in bed. I'm editing the last couple chapters I wrote for my book. How are you, James?"

"We can scratch off today. I'm sorry, Rae. I was looking forward to it."

"The pain is bad?"

Rae heard the broken sigh. "It's bad."

She felt terrible for him. "Is there anything I can do?"

"I wish there was. I really wish there was."

The situation was wearing him down and it showed in his voice. "I don't mind a lazy day watching movies. What interests you? I'll bring a few over," she offered, trying to lift his spirits.

"Rae, you don't need to do that. Go shopping. Enjoy the rare day off."

"I would rather spend it with you."

"I'll be selfish and say I would like that, too. But I'm lousy company at the moment, Rae."

"You've got cause." Rae worried her bottom lip, trying to decide what would be best. "Why don't I come over about two o'clock with a puppy and a movie."

"A puppy?" Rae could hear his smile.

"One of Margo's litter. You said yourself puppies were good medicine."

"You will be chasing it all over the house."

"Probably. Say yes."

James chuckled. "Sure, why not? I'll leave the door unlocked. Let yourself in."

The puppy that had been named Justin adored riding in the car. He sat on the passenger seat with his nose stuck out the slightly opened window, loving the motion.

Rae had done her shopping, two hours in the crowds convincing her there were better places to be on the day after Thanksgiving. She had chosen three movies at the video store, then stopped by the kennel to pick up Justin.

Last night had been yet another realization of what kind of obstacles they continued to face. James wanted to view his health as his problem, but he was wrong. It was their problem. She loved him. They were headed for a future together. The reality of the pain he faced every day was part of that future. She had seen it go into remission twice. Eventually, this episode had to go into remission as well. He was getting better, even he would admit that, even if it was occurring at a snail's pace.

She hated to see him in pain. Hated to know something she had done had contributed to that pain. The day she had realized hugging him hurt him . . . She still winced when she thought of that day. She had inadvertently done something similar again last night. He was a rugged, masculine, strong guy. Looking at him, it was hard to fathom that at times the simple actions of carrying something, shaking hands, walking, were physically painful for him to do.

God, why? I'm in love with him. I hate to see him in pain. I hate the fact there is so little I can do to help.

Thankfully, she had a leash and collar for Justin or the puppy would have wiggled himself out of her arms as she walked up the driveway to James's home. She loved this house. She loved the structural changes he had made. She would love to live in this house. She pushed open the front door, calling James's name.

"Back here, Rae."

She found him in his office working on a sketch at the drafting table. He got up from the stool, moving very stiffly.

Rae didn't comment on his pain. She squeezed his hand gently and looked at the drawing. "This is for the Grants?" They were adding another bedroom and a family room onto their ranch-style home.

"Yes." James reached over to pet a squirming Justin. "You can let him down in the house."

Rae slipped the puppy off the leash. He started exploring the room. "The sketch is very good."

"I had a few minutes to kill," James replied.

Rae could tell he wasn't satisfied with the drawing yet. "I brought three movies for you to choose from."

James motioned toward the living room, walked with her, leaning heavily on the cane to favor his left ankle. "Good choices?"

Rae smiled and told him the names of the films.

"You honestly expect me to choose?"

"Prioritize," Rae conceded. "I really want to see them all."

James laughed. "I can do seven hours of movies if you can."

"Watch me."

They ended up on the couch, Justin alternating between sitting in one or the other's lap and playing on the floor with James's rolled-up socks.

They started with John Wayne. They laughed together through most of the movie as any loud sound effect in the movie made Justin scamper for cover. He preferred burying his head under James's arm. They took a couple intermissions in the movie, Rae knowing James needed to move around frequently to keep his joints from stiffening too much.

"James, where do you keep the plastic wrap?" Rae opened yet another kitchen cabinet drawer. James had agreed to let her fix dinner as long as she simply reheated leftovers from the Thanksgiving Day meal.

"Try the second drawer to the right of the dishwasher."

"Thanks."

She came back with thick turkey sandwiches, scalloped potatoes, and two large slices of pumpkin pie.

James took the plate she offered. "I could get used to this."

Rae grinned. "Of course. Everyone likes to be waited on."

"I was referring to the food, but the service is not bad either."

Rae considered batting him with a pillow, but refrained due to the fact it might actually hurt him. "Just be glad I'm here. Without me — no movies, no puppy, no pie."

James leaned over and kissed her. "Forgiven?"

"For a kiss, I would forgive almost anything," Rae replied, grinning, at the same time, serious. She meant it.

James pointed to her plate. "Eat. I can't afford to kiss you again."

James selected the action-adventure film as the next movie. Rae was glad. She didn't need to be watching a romance at the moment.

They both laughed at the same places in the movie. Rae had seen it numerous times and still liked the way it had been plotted. It was a long movie. The ending felt good. The good guys had won.

"Are you sure you want to see all three in one day?" James asked.

It was dark outside, the credits for the movie were rolling by. Rae was tired, the puppy was asleep in her lap. But it wasn't that late. . . . "I'm game. It's one of my favorite movies."

James changed the movies.

"Come here, stretch out and get comfortable," he encouraged when he was seated again. Rae didn't need to hear the suggestion twice. She carefully settled the puppy, and stretched out on the couch, using James's lap as a pillow.

It felt good having his hand resting against her waist, occasionally brushing through her hair. It felt good to be close to him.

"Whoever thought of this script came up with a wonderful storyline," Rae said.

"Your book will make a good movie someday."

Rae looked up, surprised. "You think so? At the rate I'm going, it will never get finished, let alone find a publisher and interest a movie studio."

"You should have reserved a few hours today to work on the book."

Rae shook her head. "No. The book and the business can fight for the same time. I'm not letting the book compete with time I can spend with you."

"Rae . . ."

She cut him off. "I want to watch the movie."

She felt him sigh, but he dropped the subject. She knew it bothered him, the fact she was getting only fragments of time to work on her book. But she didn't view taking time away from their relationship to be worth the price. The book had been part of her life for three years; if it took another two years, that was the unfortunate reality. She loved days spent with James too much to want to create a tug-of-war between spending time with him and working on the book. James came first. It was that simple.

It was late when Rae reluctantly moved to go home. The puppy was coming home with her for the night.

James made sure she had her jacket on.

James rubbed the sleepy puppy under the chin. "He's going to wake you up very early in the morning."

Rae smiled. "That would be okay."

She wanted to hug him good-night, but her hands were full holding the puppy and carrying the videotapes. He had been unusually quiet for the last hour; she wished she knew what he was thinking about. It was something serious, that was obvious.

He leaned down and kissed her very gently. "Drive careful, Rae."

"Good night, James."

Chapter Ten

✝

She had carried in his groceries.

James lowered his head, his hands resting against the counter. This was not right!

The anger inside — at God, at the pain, at the unfairness of what was happening, at the lack of sleep — roiled through him.

"I don't need another mother," he snapped at Rae, taking the last sack from her as she came in from the garage. "I can put away my own groceries."

She pulled back, her eyes going wide. He watched as the light of animation gave way to confusion and deep hurt. She started to say something, stopped, then left the kitchen.

"Rae . . ."

He'd been to the doctor and then to the store and she'd been waiting for him when he got home. He was tired, in pain and frustrated with what he couldn't do. He didn't need her doing one of the few things he could do.

She didn't deserve having her head bit off because he was in a foul mood.

"Rae." He found her sitting on the couch in the living room. He lowered himself into the chair opposite her, setting the cane down. "I'm sorry. That was uncalled for."

"If I help you, you get mad. If I don't, I feel horrible."

He leaned his head back, hating the situation. He wanted her help, but resented it, too. "I know. I've been a bear with a sore head lately. I didn't mean to snap."

"Can I at least fix dinner?"

It pulled a half smile from him. "Would you settle for helping me fix it?"

She bit her lip as she sighed. "Sure. The doctor's news was bad?"

"Nothing different than last time. Wait it out." It was impossible to make light of how desperate he was to get some sustained improvement. There were few if any glimmers of hope.

Kevin was right. He had to accept the limitations and learn to live with them. But he hated it, hated the implications of a life with this pain. Hated the cost he was going to have to pay.

If he didn't recover, they didn't have a future together.

She didn't want to talk about the possibility of this pain being a permanent reality. She still believed it would fade with time. He was no longer sure.

The only thing he was certain of was that he could not burden her with it.

It was dawn. Rae looked out her office window to see the clouds turn pink on the horizon, slowly glow as the sun touched them.

She looked down at the list of her day's priorities and slowly curled her hand around the pen she held. Had it been a pencil, it would have cracked under the pressure.

There was too much to do and not enough time to do it.

It was no longer a matter of delegation, of prioritization, of managing her time better, of controlling interruptions. She was in over her head, and she had two options. She could throw away everything outside of work that was important in her life to deal exclusively with delivering the kind of investment returns her clients had the right to expect, or she could sell the business. A partnership was not going to happen. Richardson had regretfully declined last week, Walters had called her last night.

Rae looked at the list of items to be done,

looked around her office, quietly closed the schedule book.

God, I've been thinking about Psalm 37 for months now. Verse 23 says the steps of a man are from the Lord. We've been talking about this decision for a long time. It's time, isn't it?

Rae was surprised at the peace she felt.

She was selling the business.

The demons liked to come in the middle of the night. His personal ones. Doubt. Anger. Frustration. The clock beside his bed showed 2:00 a.m. The pain had ensured he had yet to fall asleep.

God, I am so angry at this pain! Why, God? Why me? Why show me a future I would love to have and then cripple me so I can't have it?

It's not fair.

I love Rae. I can't do this to her. I can't so limit her life to this level.

I know what marriage demands of people. Why put love in my heart and deny me the health I need to enjoy it? For years I have accepted being single as one of the costs to pay for serving on the mission field. Is this how You reward that sacrifice? Why, God? I don't understand.

How do I explain this to Rae? She's not going to understand and I don't have the words. She's going to see the things I can't do — mow the yard, take out the trash, carry a sack of groceries, that long list of daily obstacles I am dealing with — as minor things. But they are not. They are the tip of that iceberg of energy and responsibility necessary for a marriage to work. It can't be such a one-sided equation that she is put in a position of constantly having to give. The marriage would never survive.

Oh, God, why does the pain not leave? What caused this relapse to be stronger and more persistent than the others? Is there anything else I can do that will help? Anything else the doctors have not tried? Just lying here in bed is making my muscles burn. I can feel the joints stiffening. I know morning is going to be another adventure in agony. I am so tired of it, Lord. There is no relief. I am dreading where this is heading.

How do I tell the lady I love that I can't marry her?

Chapter Eleven

✝

"Because I've got energy and you don't, you're dumping me."

He couldn't let this disease end up affecting her health as well. And it was. Rae was burning out trying to manage the new account and make time to help him. He refused to let it happen. Today, hearing yet another cautious verdict from his doctor, he had finally realized he no longer had the luxury of assuming his health was going to improve.

James was exhausted, in more pain than he could ever remember, and she had left work to come help him do laundry. She reluctantly admitted when directly asked that she was going to have to go back to work for a few more hours when they were done. He could see the fatigue etched in her face. He knew she had her own long list of errands and tasks to do; he knew she had ceased to work on a book that was very important to her in order to be there to help him. He wanted her in his life, but he was no longer willing to have her life limited by his. It wasn't fair to her, and it was not something he could accept. It was too high a price.

"Rae, I thought I would be getting better. I'm not. It's crazy to go on with a relationship that can't go any further."

"Did you ever think I might simply like you? That I might like being with you? James, I could care less what we actually do."

"Rae, it's hard to accept help."

"Well it's hard to see you in pain, too." She paced, frustrated. "If I help you, you get mad, and if I don't, I feel horrible. It's a no-win situation."

"Which is exactly my point. Rae, we tried. It just won't work. You've got your job and the time demands of it, I've got this disease and the implications of it. You don't have time for a relationship and I don't have the energy for one. Let's face the facts and let it go. We'll still be friends."

She was crying. "James, I don't want us to just be friends."

He closed his eyes at the plea in her voice. "Rae, I'm sorry, but that is all we can be."

She didn't know where to direct the anger. At James? At God? At herself?

Rae drove, not caring where she went. Her heart was too broken to know how to process the hurt.

The napkin from the morning's fast-food restaurant coffee was tucked in her hand, wadded up, too wet to absorb any more tears. She let the rest run unchecked down her face as she drove.

Friends.

She didn't want to be just friends.

Lord, why? Why tonight of all nights?

The paperwork was beside her, the contracts to sell the business. She and James had been planning to go to dinner and she had planned to tell him about the deal after dinner. She had known he would be against the idea, would feel as if she were sacrificing her business on his account. She had known they would need time to talk it through.

It was a good offer.

For the good of their future, it had been the right decision for her to make.

They didn't have a future anymore.

Her home was up ahead, dark, quiet. Rae pulled the car into the drive, wiping away the tears. Already her eyes were burning from the salt, feeling gritty and swollen. Her headache was intense. She left the car, feeling the cold strike her wet face.

Lace was in New York. Dave was in

Dallas. She wanted her friends — needed them. Knew even if they were here, they couldn't fix the problem.

A scampering puppy met her at the door. Justin had become a permanent resident. Normally she would have scooped him up and spent thirty minutes playing with him, but tonight she greeted him, rubbed his coat and put him back down.

She went outside to the deck and tossed the contract pages onto the grill.

One strike of a match and the contract flared into a bright ball of heat, curled black and turned to ash.

She had her work and her book. She didn't have what she really wanted.

She watched the flames burn until the contract was entirely ash.

God, I let him get close, and I got hurt.

I'm tired of getting hurt.

Next time, remind me to say no when I get asked for a date.

Rae went downstairs at 1:00 a.m. to answer the doorbell. Tired of lying in bed fighting the tears, she had finally gotten up and settled in the recliner with one of her mom's books, trying to bury the pain in the old familiar words of a children's fantasy.

It was hard to read when you were crying.

Dave. He had been in Dallas. He had called her from there expecting to hear she had told James about the deal. Instead, he had heard a carefully edited explanation of the evening. He must have chartered a flight. Rae blinked against the tears.

He stepped inside.

She had never been so glad to see someone.

"You look like you could use a hug," her friend said quietly, opening his arms.

She buried herself in his strong protective arms, letting the pain finally come out. Her dreams had died tonight. It was a pain that went deeper than any loss she had ever felt before. Leo had not made a choice to leave her. James had. It stung. Deep inside her soul, it stung.

Dave held her for a very, very long time.

"He's a jerk."

"No, he's not, Lace. He did what he thought was best."

Rae didn't feel the forgiveness she expressed, but said the words again anyway. She had said them a lot in the past week, Lace was like a lioness ready to take James apart. Rae was no longer angry. She was sad, tired, licking her wounds in private.

Anger was a luxury of energy she didn't have to spend.

The funny thing was, she honestly did understand his actions. His back against the wall, not able to deal with the demands the relationship required while in such physical pain, he had ended it as gently as he could. She had been ready to do the exact same thing with her business, admit she couldn't carry the weight, sell out. Thank God she had not actually signed the pages.

"Lace, I love your company, I appreciate the lunch, but . . ."

". . . let me get back to work," Lace finished for her, getting to her feet.

"Yeah. Sorry."

Lace leaned her hands on the desk. "It's okay. As long as you come over tonight, watch a movie, eat popcorn, forget about work for at least three hours."

Rae grimaced. "Can I call you?"

Lace shook her head. "Come. That's an order from your friend. You haven't left this office for the past week."

"I'll try to be there by eight."

"If you're not, I'll kidnap you."

It was the first smile Rae had felt and meant in days. "I'll be there, Lace."

James had expected a reaction from Dave

and Lace. He hadn't expected the ice.

It began to thaw slightly as they watched him carefully set down his coffee mug, before he dropped it. The pain was intense tonight. Had it not been for the slight chance he'd see Rae, he would have passed on the get-together.

Rae hadn't come.

Lace, across from him, asked about his family. She didn't approve of what he had done, that was obvious, but she was at least being polite.

It seemed that Dave had not taken sides.

James wanted to ask how Rae was doing, wanted to hear anything about her, but neither Dave or Lace were willing to mention her name. During the past week, James had picked up the phone several times to call her, but always reluctantly replaced it. He hoped she would eventually forgive him.

Chapter Twelve

✝

"James, she's taking it pretty hard. She doesn't let many people inside her shell and she did you," Lace told him. "She doesn't understand."

Lace, knowing how bad he missed her, had finally relented, begun to call him, tell him what she knew.

Almost two weeks without seeing Rae. It was crushing him. James felt as if he had lost his right arm, so deep was the void where their friendship had been.

Christmas was drawing near and Rae was pleading the pressure of end of year work to avoid him. She had skipped the party tonight, and he had come for only one reason, to see how she was doing, to give her an early Christmas gift. He had never meant to hurt her, not this way.

They couldn't have a future together; it was for her own good that he had pulled back. But he was miserable and it didn't help to know she was also as miserable. This was for the best. It had to be. No matter how many times he stopped to consider the options, it always came down to a simple fact that he didn't have the energy for a marriage, to provide for a wife, let alone the energy to raise a family. He couldn't do it. He couldn't take away her dreams of a family, her dreams of writing, just to make his life easier. She would wear out caring for him.

He was no longer a nice, patient, optimistic man to be around. The pain had removed that pair of rose-colored glasses. The pain had taught him that he wouldn't be able to have everything he wanted. It felt like a cruel lesson, and he hated the reality, but he couldn't change it. He couldn't make the pain go away.

He wanted so badly to be well, to be fit enough to ask Rae to marry him, to build a home with her, to raise a family with her. But reality and what he wanted were a long way apart. It took energy to be in a relationship. It meant being able to at least take walks with her, carry out the trash, repair things that broke, mow the lawn, be there to take care of her when she got a cold. In the shape he was in, she would be constantly having to take care of him. He hated that reality.

But he had never meant for her to get hurt.

He needed to see her, to explain again as best he could why it had to be this way. She was still at the office, Dave had told him that. Since she was avoiding him, he would need to go to her.

He looked at the clock. There was no better time than tonight.

Dave had given him the key to the office suite, and for the first time he walked through the rooms to find them quiet, dark, silent. Her office door was open, the light spilling out into the research room.

She sat at her desk, her head in her hand, the droop of her shoulders weary, as if she felt the weight of the world pressing her down. She was walking a pen down a spreadsheet of numbers, deep in thought. Two weeks. He looked at her and wanted so badly for things to be different. He loved her so much.

"Hey, lady," he said softly, "it's awful late."

She looked up.

Her face lit up momentarily when she saw him, then clouded again. "James. What are you doing here?"

"May I come in?"

She nodded to the chairs in front of her desk, then out of consideration, moved from the chair behind the desk to one of the group in front of the desk. Not the one beside his.

"How are you?" she asked quietly.

"Four out of ten," he replied in the shorthand they had used for a long time. He studied her face, missing her, hoping something could be done to restore at least their friendship. "You look tired." It was an understatement. He hated what he saw, but knew he had contributed to it.

She grimaced. "There's been a lot of work to do," she replied.

He reached in his pocket and retrieved the gift he had hoped to give her tonight at the party. "I brought you something."

She hesitated before accepting the envelope, opening it.

He loved the smile he saw for he had the feeling she had not smiled in the past two weeks.

"Tickets to the Bulls game?"

"You need an evening away. If it turns out to be a bad day for me, Dave volunteered to take you," James said with a slight smile.

"Dave will help you have a bad day so he can go in your place," Rae replied, amused.

"Will you come?"

James watched her bite her bottom lip. "Rae, it's a simple question."

She shook her head and handed back the tickets. "Thank you, James, but no."

He felt the rejection cut deep into his heart. He did his best not to show it. He deserved it. "What if Dave is the one who takes you?" he asked quietly.

She shook her head.

"Rae, you need a break."

"I've got one. I've been working on the book in the evenings."

"When are you sleeping?"

She didn't like him pushing; he could see it so clearly in her expression. It was buried alongside an enormous pool of hurt. He had never meant to leave her with that.

She got to her feet. "James, I'm okay. Honestly. But I've got a lot of work to do."

He could hear the unsaid goodbye in her actions.

He hated this, hated this death of a friendship. "I'm sorry, Rae. I don't want it to end this way."

"Neither do I. But it has to be this way." There were tears in her eyes as she moved back to her desk.

James had never felt more helpless. "Will you call me if you change your mind about the game?"

She nodded. "Take care of yourself, James," she whispered.

"You too, Rae."

He left, feeling his heart break. He walked to his car, the tears flowing down his face, hating the disease which had cost him what he most wanted in life.

Rae tried to concentrate on her book, tried to pick up where she had left off in the story, but the page blurred and the words ran together. She wasn't going to cry anymore. She wasn't!

The tears slipped down onto the page anyway.

James had looked so tired tonight, in so much pain. She desperately wanted the right to be with him on nights like this; to be his wife, have the right to hold him, help him, be with him. Instead, she sat alone in her home, trying to distract herself with a story that would probably never be finished, let alone be published.

God, why?

It was a prayer whispered around choking sobs. She hurt so badly.

He was the man she loved, the man she so hoped would become her husband, and he had instead simply said, "I can't." Nothing in her life had ever hurt this bad. Not the death of her parents, not the death of her grandmother, not even the death of Leo.

God, why?

"James, are you sure I can't get you something?"

James reached up and softly squeezed the hand that rested on his shoulder. "Thank you, Patricia. But I'm okay."

His sister didn't believe him. James couldn't blame her. He looked and felt like something that had been flattened by a semi. "You ought to be off your feet," he cautioned.

"I'm fine."

James tugged her to a chair with a smile. "Sit."

She reluctantly did as ordered. "I feel like a beached whale."

"You look beautiful pregnant. Enjoy it."

"You're not the one who gets to feel Junior kick for the fun of it."

James laughed. The sound was rusty; he hadn't had reason to laugh for a while. "Still sure it's a boy?"

"I don't know. Emily was like this, too, active. I guess I'm willing to wait for the surprise." His sister rubbed her aching back. "You saw the doctor this morning?"

James rubbed his aching wrist. "Same

old, same old. Another anti-inflammatory medication to try. They don't have many suggestions."

"I'm sorry, James."

"I know." He wished he could stay even slightly optimistic that the pain would fade like it had done before. "It's the breaks."

"How's Rae?" Patricia asked softly.

James felt his face grow taunt. "Angry. Hurt. About what I expected."

"She'll forgive you, James."

James sighed, feeling so old. "Someday."

The office was silent. Rae rubbed her burning eyes, trying to restore her concentration. She had added the numbers three times and come up with different answers each time. She had work to do. She couldn't afford to be calling it a night at 9:00 p.m.

Her body had other plans. Wearily, she conceded the choice was no longer hers.

She closed the folders and added them to the stack at the side of her desk. Tomorrow morning. She could finish them then.

Her life was entirely this job. She had chosen to make it that. No use having a pity party over her own choices.

Her car was in the first spot in the parking lot, since she was normally one of the first people to arrive at the building in the morning. Tonight, her car was also one of only three cars left in the parking lot. She got in, tossed her briefcase and purse onto the passenger seat, flipped on her car lights.

Her body reminded her that she had not eaten since ten that morning, and she wearily gave in to the insistent demand. There wasn't much at home. She needed milk. Some ice cream wouldn't be bad, either.

Traffic was sparse.

Rae drove home, trying to pull her mind off work and think about her book, what she would write that night. Some nights it was only a page or two, but it was better to be working than to be thinking about James.

She wasn't angry at him anymore. She knew how hard the decision had to have been for him to make. She didn't necessarily want to see him again, either. Lace was upset with her because she had canceled joining them tonight. She didn't want to see James, didn't want to feel the hurt, didn't want to be reminded of what she wouldn't have. Marriage. Children.

At first, the hope had been strong that he would recover and change his mind. As the weeks were passing and reports from Lace and Dave were of no change, her hope had dwindled. She was down to Psalm 37, verse 30. God was her refuge in time of trouble.

The verse fit; it helped. She had never needed a place of refuge more deeply than she did now.

"Is Rae coming?" Dave asked.

"She pleaded work when I called," Lace replied.

Dave's mouth tightened. "This is getting ridiculous. She takes on new clients and refuses to hire more help."

James, seated on the couch, knew what Rae was doing but also felt a need to defend her. "She'll eventually pull back again, Dave. She's hurt and work is her first defense."

Dave sighed. "Any suggestions?"

"No. I wish I had one. Would you stop by her office, offer to take her to dinner? Lace says she's losing weight again."

"I'll do that. Why don't you two just get back together?"

James shifted the cane he was now forced to use all the time. "She doesn't need another burden, Dave."

"Really? Was that her decision or yours?"

Rae chose the corner store near her home to pick up milk, was disappointed with the ice cream options and ended up choosing plain vanilla.

A light freezing drizzle had begun to fall. Rae shivered as she slipped back inside the car, was grateful for the warmth. She pulled to the corner and waited for the red light to turn.

Her car was hit in the driver's door as she pulled out with a green light.

When Lace returned to the living room after answering the phone, her face was white. James felt himself bracing even before he heard her words.

"Rae's been in an accident."

Chapter Thirteen

✝

It was an indication of how badly Rae was hurt that there were two surgeons who joined them in the waiting room, both men still in surgical greens.

James watched them from his seat, his hands tightly held together, his elbows braced on his knees. He leaned forward, searching their faces for the truth. He looked at them and knew it was going to be bad.

Fear gripped his body as he read the news in the men's faces.

Dave wrapped his arm around Lace's shoulders.

"The worst injury is a fracture in the back of her neck, just above the fourth vertebra. She's in very critical condition. We've got her stabilized, but it's going to be a long night. As the swelling around her spine goes down, we'll know how much movement and sensation she'll get back. When she was brought into the emergency room, she had no sensation or movement of any kind below her neck and she was having severe trouble breathing."

"She's going to live?" Dave demanded.

The doctor hesitated.

"She's also got broken ribs, a collapsed lung, a dislocated shoulder. She's started to run a temperature. None of those injuries is life threatening, but the shock is a problem. We will know a lot more in twenty-four hours."

"She'll be out of recovery and moved to ICU in another hour," the other surgeon said. "We'll take it day by day. Don't assume the worst or the best. Reality is likely going to lie somewhere between the two."

The intensive care unit had a waiting room with couches as well as chairs, a coffee stand in the corner of the room. Dave paced, and Lace used the phone, calling friends to let them know what had happened. James sat on the couch fighting the pain and fighting the panic.

She had to be okay. She just had to be.

Rae had worked herself to the point of exhaustion, having been at the office by 5:00 a.m., not leaving until 9:00 p.m. She had stopped to buy a gallon of milk at the store on the way home. The accident had happened at a busy intersection less than four blocks from her house, her car hit on the driver's side by another vehicle. No one was quite sure what had caused the accident.

James felt like it was his fault.

She was paralyzed, she had broken ribs, a collapsed lung, a dislocated shoulder. It should have been him, not her.

His mom, Patricia, Kevin, all came to join the silent vigil. Patricia came over and hugged him. It hurt his ribs and helped his heart.

"She'll be okay, James."

James nodded, wishing he could share his sister's optimism.

It was almost two hours before Rae was moved to the ICU and they had the first chance to see her, only five minutes each hour, only one of them at a time. James didn't ask to be the first. He wanted to, but the situation was complex at best, for he carried the guilt of knowing his actions had contributed to her fatigue. Lace and Dave looked at each other and took pity on him, sending him with the nurse.

James stepped into the quiet room, afraid of the worst. Rae was in a steel brace to keep her neck still, a respirator breathing for her. They hadn't mentioned how badly her face had been bruised.

"Hey, lady," he whispered softly, fighting the tears.

He eased her lax hand into his, very gently stroked her hair. "I hear you're having a rough night, so I came to keep you company," he said softly. "Lace and Dave are here to see you, too."

He kept stroking her hair, talking softly, fighting the tears that wanted to fall. She was a mess.

He didn't care.

He didn't care if she could walk or move. He loved her. He didn't care what stuff she could no longer do.

He realized in that instant what she had meant when she said she didn't care how much energy he had. Love really did make the limitations irrelevant.

A few of the tears slipped across his smile. "Rae, I love you. Everything is going to be all right. Just keep fighting, okay?"

He tenderly brushed back the hair from her forehead, uncovering yet another ugly bruise. He tried to stop the smile that refused to be contained; it was smile or cry. "Honey, you really did do a good job this time. I don't think black and blue are your best colors," he quipped gently. "Can you open your eyes for me?"

It took her a few moments, but her eyelashes fluttered open.

He tightened his hold on her hand but realized with a sinking tightness in his chest that she could not feel it.

He touched her cheek. She could not speak with the respirator, but he could see the emotion in her eyes; the fear, the pain, the confusion. "You're going to be all right, honey. I love you and everything is going to be okay," he said softly.

Her face stiffened at the respirator and he carefully soothed out the tension. "Don't fight it, honey, your body just needs time to heal. Let it."

Slowly he saw her relax.

"That's better. Lace and Dave are here, too. We're going to keep you company tonight."

Her eyes blinked. They suddenly welled with tears and he shifted, ignoring the burning pain in his back, reaching forward with both hands to gently touch her bruised cheeks, wipe away the tears, careful to avoid the bandage on her neck. "You're going to be okay, Rae. Please, don't cry. I know it's scary, but we're here, we're not going to leave you."

The panic in her eyes . . . It scared him, because she was so desperately frightened.

She had realized she couldn't move. "Rae, you've got a small fracture just above the fourth vertebra in your neck. It's the swelling that is causing the paralysis."

Her eyes went dark.

"It's temporary, Rae. The swelling will go down. All your injuries will heal."

He held her face, held her eyes with his, until she accepted the hope he offered, until she finally released the panic and trusted him. She blinked and he very gently wiped away the tears.

"Try to sleep, Rae. I promise, we'll be here through the night. I love you."

Her eyes drifted closed, the tears still slowly trickling down her face.

Dawn came slowly, tingeing the sky with a brush of pink. James eased the coffeepot back onto the warmer plate. One of the hospital volunteers had brought in muffins and bagels. James looked at the platter. He should eat, but there was no way he could.

He carried the coffee cup with him back to the couch.

Lace was asleep.

It had been a difficult night, the waiting, the lack of news. Rae was getting worse, that was apparent. Each visit saw the temperature higher, her eyes more clouded, the distress more apparent.

He was afraid. Afraid like he had never been before in his life.

The doctors were coming in more often — a bad sign.

"Did you reach Jack?" James asked as Dave came back into the waiting room.

"Yes. The business is taken care of, at least for the next few days."

Dave looked as burned out as James felt. A night without sleep was taking its toll. He had sent his mom and sister home shortly after 1:00 a.m., asked Kevin to drive them. Patricia especially needed to sleep.

James looked at the clock. Another ten minutes before they could see Rae again.

Dave went in to see her first, they had been rotating each hour. James could see the distress on his face when he returned. He was obviously shaken.

"James, she's not doing well. I'm going to wake up Lace."

James's hand involuntarily clenched around the cane his weight rested on. Waking up Lace . . . He moved through the doorway to the ICU, needing desperately to see Rae.

He knew. As soon as he saw her, he knew.

The nurse with her finished her task,

touched his arm. "Talk to her. It will help," she said softly.

Her temperature had shot up.

She no longer opened her eyes. It wasn't because she was sleeping.

He stroked her cheek, feeling the heat radiating off her body. They were using ice to try to give her some relief.

"Rae, I know it has got to be so hard right now, to breathe, to want to fight. Rae, you need to fight. Don't let this injury win."

What did she have to fight for? A job that wore her out? A man who had walked away from her, not understanding the truth?

"Rae, I love you. Please, fight off this shock. I know you can do it."

She looked so fragile, so broken.

He was afraid that it was not only her body that was broken, but also her spirit.

James napped awkwardly in a chair throughout the morning, catching ten minutes here, twenty minutes there, enough to keep him going.

He had aged ten years in one night.

There was no improvement in her condition.

The hardest thing to accept was the fact that Rae was holding on only by a thread.

There was a flutter developing in her

heart rate, a wandering missing beat. James had seen it occur, watching the monitors, and the sight of that momentary flat line had been horrifying.

Her temperature was holding at 103 degrees.

God, I've been trying to pray for the last several hours and I simply don't have the words. My heart is breaking. She's so badly hurt. Don't take her away God. Give me another chance. Please.

He came awake with a start, someone lightly shaking his shoulder.

It was Lace.

"Sorry, James, but I thought you would want to see her."

Through the exhaustion, James saw the smile. "She's awake."

The smile widened as Lace nodded. "She's awake. The fever is down to a hundred and one."

James struggled to get up. His body rebelled at the movement, threatening to send him crashing to the floor. Lace steadied him.

"Thanks," he said, grateful for the help.

"Go see her. She's still got that look of panic in her eyes. I don't think she remembers much of what's been going on around her."

He entered her room and walked to the side of her bed. "Hey, lady. How are you doing?"

He moved into her line of sight and saw the tension in her face start to relax.

"I'm glad to see you awake," he whispered, gently stroking her cheek. She was still flushed, her body hot, but not as dangerous as it had been an hour ago.

With the paralysis and the brace holding her head, she had no movement of any kind. The respirator breathed for her, steady, constant, no variation. He could see the fear in her eyes, and the pain.

"Do you remember me saying I love you?"

Her eyes looked troubled. She had not remembered.

He smiled softly. "I love you, Rae." He brushed the hair back from her forehead, leaned forward to gently kiss her. "Keep fighting to heal. I'm not going anywhere."

"I know what you meant about pain being a malicious enemy." Her lips were white with the agony of having the dressing of the burn on her neck changed.

They had removed the respirator that morning.

James tightened his hold on her hand,

wishing she could feel it. He carefully wiped away the tears on her face. "Hang in there, the pain will ease off."

She couldn't feel ninety percent of her body and where did she get burned? Someplace she *could* feel. He hated the maliciousness of this accident.

She had slept most of the day.

He had tried to rest, trading places with Lace and Dave regularly, but it had not happened. His own body ached. He didn't care. He wasn't leaving.

"They said seventy-two hours?"

"Rae, you've got a long way to go before the swelling comes down and you know something definite. Don't borrow trouble."

"It's been almost three days, James."

"And the scans this morning showed little reduction in the swelling. Wait it out."

She tried to laugh. "I wasn't praying for patience."

He gently wiped the tears away from her eyes. She had cried more in the last three days than he had seen her do in their entire relationship. She had cause. He eased forward to kiss her forehead, wishing so hard for God to answer his prayer. "I know it's hard," he whispered. "You can make it."

"Tell me again."

"I love you. I'm always going to love you."

She was biting her bottom lip. He gently stopped her. "What do you need to ask?" He hated the pain he saw in her eyes, the uncertainty.

"Even if there is no change?" she whispered.

She had risked her heart to ask that question. James felt a tear slide down his own cheek. His finger rubbed her chin. "Even if there is no change."

Chapter Fourteen

They put the Christmas tree on the table where she could see it. It had been the nurse's suggestion — something for Rae to look at as she fought to keep her spirits up. It was porcelain, the lights blinking different colors.

Four days, and no change.

Rae was desperately afraid. They all were.

Christmas Eve last night had been a time to pray for her and hope for the best.

"I'm sorry I didn't get you anything," Rae said, breaking the tension and making the group of them laugh.

"You always were a Christmas Eve shopper," Lace replied. "Would you like me to be your hands?" she offered softly. They had brought in Rae's stocking. It was filled with little gifts. Most of them made her laugh, for they had been bought with that in mind.

The little white dog like Justin with a red heart for a tag made her cry.

"We couldn't smuggle in the puppy, so we had to improvise," James told her, brushing away the tears.

"It's very nice. Thank you," she whispered, choking on the words. "How is he?"

"Staying with Emily and Tom. Missing you."

"She moved her toes!"

James felt his heart lurch as Lace stopped in front of him. He was sitting in the ICU waiting room, weary beyond belief, fighting the grief, trying to pray. He looked at Lace and it took a moment for her words and grin to sink in. "She moved."

"She moved. Both feet. You should have seen her smile. Come on, you need to see her." Lace offered a hand and James took it, his wrist flaring in pain, his joints fighting the movement.

His smile began slowly, cautiously. He had been at the hospital for six days, had left only to change, take a shower, catch a few moments of sleep. He had never felt such a deep loss of hope. The obstacles they faced were so deep; if she didn't improve, she would need so much help that would be beyond him to provide.

She had moved.

The nurses let them enter the ICU together.

James stopped by the door, for Rae had two doctors with her. He stayed and listened as the doctors reviewed how much improvement had occurred. It was slight; she could move her toes and she had feeling in her hands. The paralysis had a long way to go before it faded, but both doctors were smiling.

James crossed over to the bedside when the doctors finished, moving into Rae's line of sight. "I hear you've got news." He slipped her hand carefully into his and squeezed it.

Her smile was wide, and there were tears in her eyes — finally tears of joy. "I can feel your hand, I can move, just a little. I was so afraid none of it would come back."

James pulled a chair over, sitting down to take the strain off his ankles.

"I was so scared."

"I know you were, Rae." He gently brushed her hair back from her face.

"You look awfully tired, James."

He smiled. "I've got a lifetime to sleep. I love you, Rae."

"I love you, too," she whispered back.

"What else do you think she will want?" It

felt uncomfortable walking through Rae's home, packing for her.

"I'll get her book. See if you can find her Bible. It's normally on her bedside table," Dave replied.

James nodded and walked upstairs, keeping a firm grip on the staircase railing. The house was exactly how Rae had left it the morning she left for work and didn't return. Dishes from dinner the night before had been left in the sink, the bathroom counter was still cluttered, and bills she had planned to mail were sitting on her desk. He had a disquieting thought; it would be like this if she had died; walking into her life as she had left it.

She had made her bed. Clothes she had considered and chosen not to wear still lay across the chair arm.

James found her Bible and her diary resting on the pillow of her bed. She must have had devotions that morning and dropped the books there. He picked up the Bible, its leather cover cool and worn. He had seen her with this Bible in her hand on so many occasions. He could see the shadow of her handprint worn into the leather from the oil of her skin. Her grip was smaller than his.

The Bible fell open to Psalm 37 showing

how frequently she smoothed this spot in the spine. Rae was one to highlight and underline and make notes.

It was comforting to get a glimpse into her real life. She could never have known someone would see her home as she left it that morning. She had devotions because she had chosen to; in the normal course of events, no one would have ever seen the evidence.

He picked up her diary, figuring she would appreciate having it as well.

The picture of Leo was gone.

James felt his hand tighten around the books he held.

The picture of Leo and the engagement ring were gone. She had done it sometime in the past, before this accident and his words "I love you."

When had she done it? When they'd started to date? In the weeks that followed?

It had to have been before he broke up the relationship — before he announced they could just be friends.

He looked at the empty spot on the bedside table and finally felt hope.

He knew how badly he had damaged their relationship. He had backed away because his health was not improving. He could feel the sinking fear in his gut that Rae might decide to do the same thing. Even though she said "I love you," it was far different from saying she would accept a relationship again, consider marrying him. She could move her toes slightly, could feel someone holding her hand. It was still a formidably long way from being totally recovered.

The doctors were being cautiously optimistic. The swelling was still there, lessening a little more each day. What they didn't know was how far the recovery would go.

He was afraid of what Rae might decide to do.

What if the accident left her in a wheelchair? What if she got mobility back in her right hand but not her left? Her spine had taken a severe blow — the fracture had cut into the nerves. What they didn't know was what would heal and what was permanently damaged. It was an ugly circumstance to consider.

He was ready to deal with it; he knew he could adapt to whatever the final outcome was. The question was, could Rae? If she remained partially paralyzed, would it be her choice this time to leave the relationship just friends?

It was difficult, watching physical

therapy. She was out of intensive care, in a private room in the rehabilitation wing of the hospital. The paralysis persisted. The swelling still lingered. There was no determining which muscles in her back, arms and legs obeyed her wishes and which ones still did not get the message to move.

The broken ribs hurt. She was constantly fighting a headache. Because she wasn't able to move easily, her body throbbed with pain from lying in one position for too long.

James felt for her and wished there was something he could do.

He sat on the far side of the room and watched as the physical therapist worked on helping her get motion in her arms. He could see the strain on Rae's face as she tried to coordinate the muscles in her shoulders and upper arms to get the movement she wanted. It was difficult — lying flat on your back, head in a brace to prevent your neck moving, knowing you had to battle to raise your arms.

After fifteen minutes the therapist declared the day a success and spent several minutes talking with a discouraged Rae to explain the improvements that were occurring.

James could see the improvement, too. Rae was getting better. It was slow, but it was definitely there.

After the therapist left, James moved back to Rae's bedside. "You are getting better," he confirmed.

She wanted to reply with something sharp, but bit back her words. James couldn't blame her for the bad mood.

"Would you like to get some sleep, talk for a while, have me pick up reading where I left off?" he asked, keeping his voice neutral.

She sighed. "Finish the book."

James studied her face, finally nodded. He picked up the suspense novel he had been reading to her, pulled the chair back to her bedside. "Is the mirror angle okay?"

"Yes."

She hated the mirror. Positioned over her, it let her see the room while she was flat on her back. She really hated it. James reached over and gently squeezed her hand, didn't let go of it as he used one hand to find the page they were on in the book. He began reading.

It took her several minutes, but she turned her hand over to grip his.

Rae was able to move now, but only with great care. The physical therapist had had her on her feet yesterday, a reality that had caused her an immense amount of vertigo. The exhaustion after therapy had caused her to sleep through the afternoon. James had sat with her, reading a book, watching for any signs of the nightmare returning.

She had been dreaming about the accident recently, waking terrified, reliving the moment she had turned her head and seen the headlights right there, the instant before the car had slammed into her driver-side door. She had no memory of the accident past that point; didn't remember the emergency room, nor much from the first couple days in the ICU. James wished her memory had erased those first few moments before the accident as well.

The first time the dream had happened, her heart rate had jumped to almost one hundred sixty beats per minute in only a few seconds. The nurse had seen it happen and shaken her awake. The doctors told her the dream would fade in intensity with time. James preferred to be there to shake her awake rather than let her complete the dream.

"She's bored."

James laughed at Lace's conclusion, joining her at the hospital cafeteria table for a cup of coffee. "I brought the reference books she asked for with me. That should help serve as a distraction."

Rae was healing, feeling better, fighting to regain motion, mobility, strength. She was fighting her way back to health.

"I hear she goes down to the physical therapy room today," Lace commented.

James carefully picked up his coffee mug, knowing his hands might drop it if he didn't concentrate. He nodded. "They want to get her relearning to walk."

"Did the doctors say what yesterday's MRI results were?"

"The swelling below the fracture point is down but it's not gone. At least that implies more improvement is still likely."

The sunlight woke her up. Rae lifted her right hand into her line of sight, flexed the fingers into a fist, pleased to simply watch the movement.

She had grown accustomed to these quiet moments. It was early. Soon the nurse and physical therapist would be in, the steel locking pins would be turned and she would be mobile again, her neck held straight by a smaller brace.

She breathed in deeply, let it out slowly.

There were a few benefits to a severe accident. She got to lie in bed for a good portion of the day, nap, read, talk to friends. She had the strength and energy of a newborn kitten.

She knew what James felt like now.

Concern for how the business was doing tensed her body and she forced the thought away. She wasn't going to worry about something she had little control over. Jack was there. Her staff were good. Dave was going in each day for a couple of hours.

She touched her hand to her face, exploring how far the swelling had come down. She had nearly broken her jaw. It still ached.

"Good morning, Rae."

She smiled at the voice of her favorite nurse. "Good morning."

A few seconds later, the face connected with the voice appeared in her line of sight.

"Breakfast is coming."

"I'm hungry," Rae remarked, surprised.

Her new friend laughed. "Your body is letting you know it's tired of IVs."

Rae held her breath as the pins were released and she was once again mobile. It felt great to be free of the large brace, but also scary. Her neck was still fragile; a fall could paralyze her for life.

The nurse helped her dress in sweats, ease back onto the bed. She was grateful physical therapy was not for another hour and a half. It was hard, knowing she should be able to do so much more, to accept the fact that her body could not do it yet.

God, I understand so much better the frustration James must feel. It's the frustration of all the little things. The fact I have to concentrate to be able to take even a single step. The fact I can't put on a pair of shoes. The fact I can't reach the book I want to read without first carefully maneuvering to get in position. The fact I get tired so easily.

"Hey, lady. Like some company?" It was a soft question from her left.

Rae turned carefully, smiled. "I was just thinking about you."

James crossed the room. "Good thoughts, I hope."

"Hmm." She watched carefully as he moved, was grateful that his pain appeared to be under control this morning. He looked like he had finally had a decent night of sleep. She had been worried about him.

He kissed her good-morning. She was reluctant to end the kiss, a fact that made him laugh. "You taste minty," he remarked, reluctantly easing away. He sat down in the chair beside her bed.

She wrinkled her nose. "Toothpaste."

He grinned. "Whatever."

She loved his smile. She loved the fact he chose to spend his days with her.

★ ★ ★

"What, no James?"

Rae had gotten adept at using the mirror above her bed, finally accepting its reality. "Hi, Lace. I sent him home." It was late and she was flat on her back, not going to be moving again until morning.

Her friend appeared in her line of vision. "I know, I'm just teasing. I saw him in the lobby."

Rae smiled. She loved James and Dave, but there were times when a girlfriend was the one who really mattered. "He looks good, doesn't he?"

"Dave or James?"

Rae chuckled. "Yes, I noticed the change in Dave, too. James."

"I think the new medication is helping. He's in less pain."

"I think so, too. Have you and Dave been dating?"

"Do you expect me to kiss and tell?"

Rae grinned. "Absolutely."

"He brought lunch over yesterday. Yeah. I think we're really dating."

"This is good."

"This is murder. I can never tell when he's pulling my leg and when he's serious."

Lace pulled a chair over, settled into it, adjusted the mirror for Rae. "I bought the baby gift you wanted for Patricia. I had it wrapped for you. I'll leave it in the second drawer of the chest, with your purse."

"Thank you, Lace."

"No problem. It was fun to wander through the baby clothes. They've got some cute fashions."

Rae groaned.

"What?"

"I just had a vision of your children, Lace. Remember kids like to play in the dirt."

"I'm not planning to have children."

Rae looked at her; her friend smiled. "Okay, so the thought has crossed my mind a few times. Anything else you need? I'll swing by on my lunch hour tomorrow."

"Thanks, Lace. I can't think of anything else."

"Then I'll see you tomorrow," her friend promised.

"All right, Rae!"

Sweat was dripping from her body. She stood at the far end of the walkway, gripping the handbars to keep herself upright. James could see the muscles in her arms quiver with the excursion.

Her smile told its own story.

The physical therapist helped her turn

and carefully sit down in the wheelchair he brought over.

Dave handed her a towel.

"You made it the distance, Rae."

James pushed himself to his feet, using the cane to steady his weight, relieve the pain in his ankles. "Another couple of days and you'll be doing stairs."

Rae grinned. "Of course."

The session over for the day, Dave pushed her wheelchair back to her room where the nurse kicked them out so Rae could have a shower and change clothes.

James took advantage of the time for a little physical therapy of his own, a walk around the hospital floor. It was hard to walk any distance, and the improvements he could see were scarce — a little less pain, a little more flexibility, but he kept to the daily routine. He was determined to be able to do ten laps in the pool this month.

"How is Rae's business doing, Dave?"

Dave grimaced. "Not good. I've been dreading her questions. Jack can manage for a few more days, maybe a few weeks, but it is becoming apparent how badly Rae needs to be back setting the direction."

"She can't."

Dave looked annoyed. "I know that. I also know she will kill me if the business loses too much ground."

The question was raised by Rae an hour later, as she sat in the hospital bed, the end raised to let her sit up. She wanted to know how Jack was doing.

Dave told her the truth.

James, sitting on the other side of the bed, reached forward and captured one of her hands, held it, stroked the back, tried to distract her. She stayed focused on Dave.

"Call Gary and ask if he'll loan us York for four weeks," she finally requested. "York reviewed our books when we wrote the contract to sell the business. He's Gary's right-hand man."

James froze. She had a contract written to sell the business?

"I'll call him when I get home," Dave promised.

James looked at the profusion of flowers sitting on the windowsill, his thoughts in turmoil. She had gotten as far as a contract to sell the business? When had this happened? The thought made him sick. She loved her work. It was followed by a worse thought. Had she done it because of him?

He eased her hand from his. "I'm going to get a soda. Would you two like anything?" He needed to get out of this room.

They both declined.

She had been planning to sell the business. James tried to absorb that fact as he walked the halls to the vending machine.

Her business was more than a career for Rae. It was part of who she was, just as being a builder was an intrinsic part of who he was. She had been planning to walk away from it?

He had come to the point where he was willing to accept that they could have a future together even with the limitations he faced. But he had been thinking about practical sacrifices that could make it possible. A live-in housekeeper. Limiting the type of activities they planned. He had never envisioned the sacrifice of her career.

Everything in him rebelled at the thought of her sacrificing her career, selling the business, for him.

He slammed his fist against the pop machine when the can refused to drop all the way to the slot. He gasped at the pain that coursed through his wrist, elbow and shoulder.

Reality.

He *hated* this disease.

She was working on her book.

James paused in the doorway to her room, watching her. She was able to be out of bed for longer and longer periods of time now. Sitting in the chair by the window, using the bed as a table to spread out her materials, she was writing on a legal pad of paper, her concentration intense.

He loved her.

He loved seeing her like this, absorbed in her work.

The latest MRI had shown the swelling was gone. The paralysis that had been lingering in some of her muscles had finally faded. She had to move slowly, she had to concentrate on her actions, her strength and stamina had a long way to go, but the doctors were now talking about a full recovery being probable. Lace had brought in a cake so they could celebrate the news.

James quietly came into the room, set down the newspaper he had brought in for her.

Rae looked up, smiled. "How's Patricia doing?"

James took a seat, grateful to get off his feet. "Contractions are now every four minutes."

Rae set aside the pad of paper and glanced at the clock. "Six hours. But she's having a wonderful time."

"She kicked me out of the room," James replied, ruefully.

Rae laughed. "Poor boy."

"Emily and Tom are pleading for a chance to see you. Care to take a stroll downstairs?"

"Sure."

She looked at him, helpless. "Can you do my shoes?" With the brace, shoes were still impossible to do on her own.

James found the tennis shoes, knelt down, smiled at her as he tweaked her socks. "I think I kind of like you just a little bit helpless."

She swatted his shoulder. "Don't get used to it. It's temporary." She giggled as he tickled her left foot, tried to pull it back. "Behave, James."

He put on her shoes, tied the laces. He got up, braced his arms on her chair, leaned forward and kissed her. He loved her blush. "Come on, lady. Time to go get smothered by the family."

Emily and Tom had drawn pictures for her of Justin so that she could see they were taking good care of her dog. Rae gratefully sat down on the sofa James led her to, then turned her attention to the children. Excited about a new baby, they gave Rae a blow-by-blow account of how their mom had gone into labor while making breakfast.

His new niece was born at seven-thirty that evening. James stood beside Rae at the glass to the nursery, his arm around her waist, looking with her at the sleeping infant.

"She's beautiful."

James turned and leaned around the brace, softly kissed Rae's forehead, comforted by the fact she was with him. "Yes." They would have children of their own someday. He looked back at the sleeping infant. He wanted to be a dad. He wanted to be Rae's husband.

Rae settled carefully down on the couch, her muscles trembling at the expense of energy it had cost her to reach this point. Dave had a careful grip on her arm to make sure she didn't stumble.

She was home.

They had decorated. There were streamers, a cake, a big Welcome Home sign stretched across her entertainment center. Rae had never felt more cherished.

"Okay?"

Rae nodded in reply to the concerned query from James. She was exhausted, but that was to be expected. It was her first substantial trip since the accident. She was still trying to relax muscles that had tensed at the experience of riding in a car again.

James helped Rae off with her jacket. It caught on the neck collar she now wore and he carefully eased her forward, sliding his hands around to free the jacket.

Rae wanted to bury her face against his chest and just be held for a very long time. She missed being in his arms. It was the fatigue as well as the reality that she was finally home that was bringing the tears.

"Hey, what's wrong, honey?" The soft endearment made her catch back a sob. His hands gently gripped hers.

"I'm okay."

"Sure you are," Dave said lightly, tucking a handkerchief in her hands. "We're glad to have you home."

She sniffed back the tears. "I'm so glad to be here."

Lace was the practical one. "Here, this should help. One homemade, chocolate fudge shake."

Rae laughed and accepted the tall shake Lace had prepared. "Thank you, Lace."

"Dave, make yourself useful, go rescue the luggage," Lace told him.

Dave tweaked her hair, but did as she asked.

James settled down on a sofa beside Rae,

very conscious of the fact he didn't wanted her trying to turn her head and strain her neck. "Come here," he urged softly, guiding her down to rest against his side. His ribs ached at the pressure and he didn't care. She was home and she was mobile and he loved her. The limitations they both faced were going to be overcome, somehow, someway.

"James?"

"Hmm?"

"I'm going to fall asleep on you."

His smile was gentle. "Go right ahead, Rae. I'll just drink your shake."

He felt her laughter.

"Rae, what was it like when your parents died?" James asked.

The question surprised Rae and she turned slightly. They were sitting on the couch in her living room watching the credits of a movie go by. She was almost asleep, resting comfortably against his shoulder, his arm around her waist, an afghan thrown across her legs. "Scary. Why do you want to know?"

"Curious, I guess. You never talk about them."

Rae let her eyes close again, too tired to fight the pull of sleep. "I remember my mom's friend Gloria came and got me from school. I remember wanting to go to my bedroom and find my doll, the one Mom had made for me. It's kind of a blur."

"What do you remember about them?"

"I remember them as being nice, loving, fun. When I got home from school, Mom would take a break from working on her book to join me in the kitchen and share a snack, normally cookies she had baked that morning. She wore perfume I really liked and used to braid my hair for me. Dad I remember as this big guy who used to pick me up and make me laugh. He liked to play checkers and read me stories."

James squeezed her hand. "Thanks."

She reluctantly pushed herself up, her hand going to protect her ribs.

"I'm sorry the ribs still hurt so bad," James said, his hands helping support her movements.

"So am I. I miss getting a hug," Rae said ruefully.

Justin was asleep on the floor in front of the couch. Rae eased over so she could get up without disturbing him. "Thanks for coming over tonight."

She sensed rather than saw James's disappointment with her remark. He didn't say anything. She knew her decision to keep some distance between them was bothering him. She didn't have the luxury right now of giving him the commitment he wanted.

"Lace said she was bringing you over dinner tomorrow night?"

Rae nodded.

"Then I guess I'll see you Thursday to give you a ride to the hospital. Noon okay?"

"I can call a cab, James."

"Physical therapy is tough enough without worrying about transportation, too. I can work at a table there just as well as I can at home."

There was no way she was going to win the discussion. Rae nodded. "Noon will be fine. Thank you."

He kissed her at the door, a lingering kiss that was touched with regret. "Sleep well tonight, Rae."

"You too," she said softly.

She turned off the porch light after his car pulled out of the driveway, walked carefully upstairs. Her muscles still quivered when the fatigue was bad, threatening her balance.

God, please help James understand. I don't want to get hurt again. I'm too beat up to be able to handle a marriage. I don't know what I'm going to do about work. Please, help James understand. I can't be what he wants, not right now. I regret that, but it is the reality.

"Rae, you're keeping your distance and you really don't need to. James isn't looking for a hostess, housekeeper and cook."

Lace was over, helping Rae clean house.

Rae could do some of the picking up, load the dishwasher, but doing the laundry, mopping the floor, cleaning the bathroom, vacuuming — they were all still beyond her stamina.

They were working together on the kitchen, having finished the upstairs earlier. Rae lifted the corner of a Tupperware lid, suspicious of what might be lurking inside. She was cleaning out the refrigerator. "Lace, I know that. But just the logistics of planning a wedding, setting up house together, creating a workable routine are beyond me right now."

"So have a long engagement. Rae, he's miserable."

Rae set yet another container of spoiled food to discard in the sink. She had to lean heavily against the counter to wait for the pain in her back to subside. The accident had left her with a whole new appreciation for how much she had taken her body for granted. "He wants me at his place so he can take care of me." She breathed out in relief as the pain subsided, carefully reached for the next item on the refrigerator shelf.

"Is that so bad?"

Rae wrinkled her nose at something that was now green. "Yeah."

Kevin hesitated, holding the sledgehammer. "James, are you sure you want to do this?"

James closed his eyes, pinched the bridge of his nose, thought about it, reconsidered for about the ninth time. He nodded. "I'm sure."

Rae was going to need a walk-in closet. It was a minor detail, but it was important. He wanted her to feel at home here . . . if, no, *when* they had a future together.

He had to keep that hope alive.

He was incredibly worried that she was going to continue to keep her distance, not allow the relationship to go forward. She was not willing to let him get close while she was less than fully recovered. She fought the muscles that refused to do her bidding. She fought a body that ached with pain. How well he understood her motivations — a misplaced belief that love would not knowingly place her burden on him. It was the same thing he had done to her.

They were both wrong.

He just had to convince her of that.

Somehow he had to find a way to get her to trust him again, risk a relationship, despite her limitations, despite his.

It took all the faith he had to hold on to that hope.

Kevin knocked out the wall.

"Rae, can I come in?"

James saw her move to rise from where she lay on the couch. "No, don't get up."

He joined her in her living room, took a seat across from her, lowered his cane to the floor. Rae did not look pleased to see him. James chose to ignore it. Justin came over to greet him. He reached down to gently tug the puppy's ears. "Hard day?"

She ran her hand through her hair. "Lace and I went grocery shopping. I don't think I'll do that again soon."

James could see the tremor in her hand from the fatigue. "Some days you will have more energy than others. It will improve with time."

"I called it quits before we got to the ice cream. Now I wish we had started at the frozen foods and worked toward the vegetables, rather than the other way around."

James understood exactly what she meant. "I was going to see if you wanted to go out this evening, but I'll ask that another night. I'll fix us dinner here."

"You don't need to do that."

Interesting tone. He hadn't heard this one before. "I'm going to anyway," he replied, his voice neutral but determined. "Would it help to nap for a couple hours, shake the fatigue?"

"Probably. I don't want to."

James grinned, he couldn't help it. "Rebellion. This is good."

Rae laughed against her will.

James walked into her kitchen only to find it was a mess. It made him stop, rather stunned; he turned and looked back to the other room, frowning heavily. She was hurting a lot more than she was willing to let on. The rebellion must have begun earlier in the day. Lace would have instinctively moved to clean the kitchen for her. It was not like Rae to toss her best friend out of the house and it would have taken that to get Lace to leave.

James poured her a glass of juice and brought it to her. "Want me to dial Lace so you can apologize?"

She looked rather mutinous as she took the glass. "It's a private fight."

He didn't move from his position standing beside the couch. She felt miserable, it didn't take a rocket scientist to see that; miserable and close to tears, and angry at the entire world. "Her work, home or cell phone number?"

"Home," Rae finally said softly.

James found the cordless phone on the third step of the staircase, and also brought her a box of tissues.

"Lace? It's James. Rae would like to talk to you."

Lace sounded as if she had been crying, a fact that made James all the more troubled. James handed Rae the phone, set the tissue box within her reach, and left the room to give her some privacy.

It took about twenty minutes to get the kitchen back in shape. After an inspection of the refrigerator contents, he settled on broiled fish for dinner.

He heard her come to the doorway and quietly set the phone down on the counter. He gave her a moment before he looked up from the asparagus he was cutting. She looked awful after she had been crying. "Everything okay now?" he asked softly, hurting for her.

She nodded. Sniffed. "What did you find?" Her voice was husky.

"Broiled trout, baked potato, asparagus. Sound okay?"

"Yes."

She sounded so incredibly . . . sad. Everything wasn't okay, she was just stuffing the pain. He set down the knife and dried his hands. She was resting against the doorjamb, her hand cradling her ribs, her energy spent. He tipped her chin up, studied her face, saw so much pain in her eyes. He put his arms around her and pulled her gently against him, taking her weight, easing her head down against his chest. He held her stiff frame and gently rubbed her back. Her body finally softened against him.

He felt the first sob ripple through her. "You must hate me!"

The emotion coming from her made him flinch even though he had known it was likely. "I don't hate you. I love you," he said calmly. "You're just tired, honey, that's all," he reassured quietly, threading his fingers through her hair. She was exhausted way past the point she could function.

It took a focused effort of all his own reserves, but he leaned down and picked her up. Upstairs was out of his possibility, so he carried her into the living room. He held her through the bout of tears, until the emotion ran its course and she finally cried herself to sleep.

He made her as comfortable on the couch as he could, quietly reassured Justin, and went to fix himself a sandwich. He wasn't going anywhere.

The phone rang. James caught it before the second ring, checking carefully to see if it had woken Rae. It was Dave. James carried the phone with him to the kitchen. "What's up?"

"I'm at Lace's place. How's Rae doing, James?"

"She'll be fine," James assured him with a confidence he didn't totally feel. "She just got overtired and her ribs are really hurting."

"Lace said Rae tripped on the stairs when she was carrying in the groceries. That was what triggered the argument, apparently. I gather she's still refusing to see the doctor?"

James's hand tightened on the phone. "Rae didn't mention she fell," he replied. His voice was level, but he could feel the anger building inside him. That lovable, crazy, irresponsible lady. She could be really hurt and she hadn't said anything.

He left the phone on the counter after saying goodbye to Dave and strode with purpose back into the living room.

"Rae, there are times I really regret you are so stubborn," he whispered softly, tucking the afghan around her. He sighed and debated what he should do.

Let it go. It wasn't worth a fight.

She stirred shortly after 10:00 p.m. Without being asked, he handed her two aspirin.

"Thank you."

He sat down beside her on the couch and gently brushed her hair back from her face. "You need to eat something, Rae. Feel up to it?"

She seemed surprised when she nodded. "I'm hungry."

He smiled. "Good."

She moved to get up, winced.

"Ribs hurt?" he asked.

She looked up at him sharply and reluctantly nodded. She wanted to know if he knew about her fall but she wasn't going to ask him. He slid a hand under her elbow and carefully helped her sit up.

"I'm sorry it's so late."

"Don't worry about it. I've been reading a good book."

She looked over to the chair he had been sitting in, looked back at him. He had been reading her recently written chapters of the manuscript.

"Are they any good?"

He smiled. "Yes."

He resumed fixing the dinner that had been interrupted hours before. He soon heard her move through the house, and then he heard water running in the bathroom.

She came back with her face washed, her hair brushed. She helped him set the table.

He broiled the trout to the point it flaked apart, found sour cream and chives for the baked potatoes. It was a quiet meal, Rae asking only a few questions about his day. James was content to sit and watch her when he finished his dinner before her. He was glad to see she had meant it when she said she was hungry, and especially glad to see she ate a decent amount.

She helped him carry dishes from the dining room back to the kitchen when they were done eating.

He was reaching for the dish soap to clean the broiler when she paused his movements, resting her hand against his forearm. "Thank you, James."

He studied the serious expression in her eyes, then he smiled. The mood needed to be lightened around here. He ruffled her hair. "You're welcome."

He hummed softly as he washed the pans and she cleared the rest of the table.

"I didn't crack a rib, I'm sure of it."

He looked up from the pan he was rinsing off. "An X ray could tell you that for certain." He didn't know what he wanted to do, accept her opinion or push the matter.

She shrugged. "I'm clumsy these days, I pick up bruises."

He understood instantly, the moment he saw that shrug.

She was embarrassed.

She was embarrassed about the fact she was not as steady on her feet as she had been before.

"I'll buy you a cane," he replied lightly. "What's your favorite color?"

She wrinkled her nose at him. "Remind me not to come to you for sympathy."

He tugged her over with one hand. "You'll get sympathy, even empathy. Just not pity." He kissed the tip of her nose. "Deal?"

She kissed him back, her arm sliding around his waist. "Deal."

She adapted to limitations better than he did.

James watched Rae carry in her briefcase from the car, noticed the way she moved, using the cane he had bought her to keep her balance as she came up the steps. The unsteadiness was not improving with time, was still made worse with fatigue. James was worried about her going back to work, but also dreading the options she was considering.

They had spent the morning installing a second handrail for her staircase, then she had gone to meet Gary, Dave and York for lunch, while he painted the trim.

He held open the front door for her.

She smiled as she got to the top of the stairs, slightly out of breath. "Thanks."

"You're welcome."

She paused at the bottom of the stairs. "This looks nice, James."

James agreed. The fresh coat of paint looked good. "I was just cleaning the brushes," he remarked, moving back to the kitchen. Rae joined him. "How did the lunch go?" he asked, turning back on the water.

Rae found a cold soda on the bottom shelf of the fridge and offered him one also. When he nodded, she opened it for him, then set it down on the counter beside him. She leaned against the cabinets beside him. "Will you really be upset with me if I sell the business?"

James didn't know how to answer that question. He hated the idea, but he certainly understood why she was considering it. "I wouldn't want you to do it because of me, Rae," he finally said.

She nodded, staring at the soda can for a long time. "The business doesn't leave time for a relationship, James. That's the bottom line of it. I have seen you more since the accident than I did for all the months before it."

She sighed and turned so she could touch his arm. "You still want to be a builder, but the illness says you can't right now. For the first time, I'm facing a limitation that says the business may not be the best thing for me to do. I want to sell the business so I can avoid the fatigue, so I can continue to have time to write. But I have to be honest, our relationship is also one of the reasons I want to sell. I don't want to give up my time with you."

James dried his hands, reached over and pulled her into a hug, careful of her healing ribs. "Rae, forget what I said in the past about your schedule and my energy. I'm not going anywhere. I love you. Do you really want to sell the business? Are you going to regret it in six months?"

Her hands slipped up to his shoulders. "I

really want to sell the business."

"Then sell it." He leaned down and kissed her. "It *will* make a honeymoon easier to schedule," he offered. James watched her blush and found it endearing. He tipped her chin up with one finger, unable to contain his soft laughter. "Rae, I've just been waiting for you to recover before I hit you with my timetable. Marry me. I've got the chapel reserved for the twenty-fifth."

She pushed away from him. "Four weeks?"

"See any reason to wait?"

"Besides a dress, invitations, flowers and the rest . . . no."

He leaned down and kissed her again, felt her hands curl into his shirt as she leaned into him. He reluctantly broke the kiss so they could breathe. "Good. Lace, Patricia and my mom will help with the arrangements."

Her arms slid around his waist so she could carefully hug him. "I can't believe you already reserved the chapel."

He chuckled. "I reserved it for the last Saturday of every month for the rest of the year," he assured her. "You're going to marry me."

He felt her laughter. "Were you nervous I would say no?"

"With Lace and Dave around? It was never a possibility." He smiled as he brushed her hair back from her face. "But Dave figured you might play hard to get."

She leaned back. "Did he?"

"Now Rae, go gentle with him. I figure his turn is coming with Lace."

"Absolutely."

"I love you, Rae. I'm sorry it took an accident to make me realize what I was walking away from."

She gently traced his face with her hand, her expression serious. "It's okay. I understand better what it is like to have good days and bad days. If you can put up with my cooking, I can adapt to a slower pace of life and quiet evenings."

"You're being kind."

"No, I'm not. I love you."

James kissed her. "Not as much as I love you."

Rae grinned and rested her hands on his chest. "How much do you love me, on a scale of one to a hundred?"

James considered the question, smiling at her. "Maybe . . . about ninety-nine."

"What?"

She giggled as he teased her with another kiss.

"I still love Africa," he replied, being fair.

"Would you show it to me someday? Your clinics and your kids?"

James took his time with the next kiss. "It would be my pleasure."

Dear Reader,

Thank you for reading *God's Gift*. It holds a special place in my heart as my second book published. This was a good story to write, for it reaffirmed hope that love can overcome any challenge. Everyone faces unexpected troubles in life, and how we respond and cope is one way we show our faith. God is still in control.

I would love to hear from you. You can find me online at: www.deehenderson.com, e-mail: dee@deehenderson.com or write me care of Steeple Hill, 233 Broadway, Suite 1001, New York, NY 10279.

Sincerely,

Dee Henderson

About the Author

Dee Henderson is the author of two romance novels and two series of romantic suspense novels. Her books have won a host of awards, including the prestigious RITA® Award, the Christy Award and the National Booksellers Best Award, and she has been a three-time finalist for the ECPA Gold Medallion Award for Fiction. She lives in Illinois.